For Elijah and Gabriel: OK, so you might not
be able to read this quite yet, but you're the reasons
why I wrote every last word.

THE
DARK

BOOK 2 OF THE DEAD

DAVID GATWARD

A Catalogue record for this book is available from the British Library

ISBN 978 0 340 99970 7

Typeset in Caslon by Avon DataSet Ltd,
Bidford-on-Avon, Warwickshire

Printed and bound in Great Britain by
CPI Bookmarque Ltd, Croydon, Surrey

The paper and board used in this paperback by Hodder Children's Books are
natural recyclable products made from wood grown in sustainable forests.
The manufacturing processes conform to the environmental regulations
of the country of origin.

Hodder Children's Books
A division of Hachette Children's Books
338 Euston Road, London NW1 3BH
An Hachette UK company
www.hachette.co.uk

'. . . out of the abysses between the stars swept chill currents that made men shiver in dark and lonely places.'

H. P. Lovecraft, *Nyarlathotep*

'Get busy living, or get busy dying.'

Stephen King, *The Shawshank Redemption*

⚜️ PROLOGUE ⚜️

It could smell blood and flesh. And it wanted to burrow into it, like a worm into an apple.

The creature had only the faintest of memories of what it was to be alive. But that had been so long ago that the memories were no longer images, simply sensations; like phantom pain after an amputation. Yet it could remember the things it had lusted for. It made it breathless to even think about them.

What it had been, man or woman, old or young, it had no idea at all. It could summon up a faint recollection of pain around its neck, but nothing more than that. It had tried to work out what this pain meant. Perhaps it had been hanged? Beheaded even? But it had never discovered anything deep inside, no clue. Nothing. And it had changed so much over the years, into something so far

1

beyond what it had looked like or been, that even a reflection would not have given enough of a clue.

But its basic instincts hadn't changed. Or its tastes. These drove it forward, licking and sniffing the air. It knew only the thirst that could not be quenched, for true *life*. Blood was pulling it forward. It would find the body that it coursed through, slip inside and *live*!

It just had to get to it before anyone – *anything* – else did . . .

As it shuffled and scuffled forward, it couldn't shift a dull sense of confusion. How could the smell of blood be in this place? Everything was dead, fresh blood did not belong. Perhaps it was a gust from the other side? New arrivals of fresh-faced Dead often brought with them the faintest of smells of the Living. But that always faded so quickly. Yet this . . . it wasn't fading at all . . .

The house was cracked and broken; black brick and stone and shattered glass, like a building slammed by an earthquake. But the creature wasn't concerned; everything looked like that here. It slipped forward, glided up the path to the remains of a front door. The garden was dead earth and dust, dried and split like sunburned mud or scorched, blackened skin.

Glancing back to the street to check it wasn't being followed, the creature eased through the door: a gaping mouth of sharp, broken teeth, the thick wood planks split and charred. The hallway swept round past a door on the left leading to a room at the front of the house, and to a staircase that pulled itself up to the first floor on a rotten, crumbling banister, forever caught in its last moment before total collapse. A death freeze.

The creature paused here for a moment. Something in this place was not right. It could smell the body stronger now than before, almost hear its heartbeat, and it was coming from further on and below the house. A cellar perhaps? This was no wisp of life from the other side. It was a body – of that it was sure. Real and soft and warm. Juicy. And it was here. In the land of the Dead. Someone had been past this way before, and very recently. Someone *alive*. Someone *walking*. A body was strange enough, but a living person actually walking in this place? Surely it was mistaken . . .

The creature ignored these nagging thoughts and turned away from the stairs to face another door. It swung uselessly on one hinge, fading carpet split with mould just visible in the gloom beyond. The hallway turned left, along the side of the stairs and round to a room with an upturned table and chairs, all broken; smashed crockery littering the floor. But the smell wasn't coming from there. It was coming from an opening under the stairs that led down into a dry, heavy darkness.

The creature slid into the black, drooling an oily slick to the floor, anticipating the moment it would find the body and push itself into the flesh.

Darkness gave way to a room of smashed shelves and desks, all covered with the dusty remains of clocks. A corner of the room reeked of rancid wine and the creature saw a mound of broken bottles. There was an opening in the far wall and steps faded downwards. It followed them to a cavern empty but for the crumbled remains of a few coffins. In the far wall lay another opening. The creature almost skipped with excitement. Here it was! Yes, this was it!

Now it found itself in another cavern, larger than the last. The room was lit strangely and at its centre lay a mangled and wrecked mess of twisted metal. The creature had no idea what the metal thing was or could have been before it had been destroyed. But whatever it was, it shimmered a little, like it was on the other side of a pool of water.

The creature then heard breathing; the sweet sound of one of the Living was just footsteps away. It turned and saw the body lying against the cavern wall, covered in rubble and dust. It looked young, male. It looked . . . perfect.

It ghosted across the floor to the body, leant down so close it could taste the boy's breath, then opened its own black mouth. In a few moments the body would belong to it. It would seep inside, take over completely, and the whole thing would be a delicious ecstasy.

Then something fell through the shimmering light around the wreck of metal at the centre of the cavern. And when the creature saw what it was, it almost screamed with delight.

1

ꙮ SULPHUROUS STENCH ꙮ

The ground came up Ferarri-fast. Too fast for Lazarus Stone to stop himself falling and slamming into it like a sack of coal dropped from a wagon. It chinned him hard, split his cheek, bloodied his eye, and – bright light of pain – broke a tooth.

He rolled on to his back with a moan. His head found itself resting on soft rags. When Lazarus looked closer, he saw they were clothes, old ones ragged and torn and stinking of mould and earth. Where the hell was he?

Lazarus peeled his eyes open, but all they caught was darkness. It was everywhere. Pushing himself on to his elbow, he blinked sweat. His ragged black fringe felt icy cold against his forehead and the back of his neck. And just what the hell was he wearing? He sat up, pulled at his clothes; some of the material crumbled in his fingers. An old jacket, trousers, riven with rot and mould and shimmering with a faint crisping of ice. They stank too, like the pile of clothes next to him. Underneath the tattered rags, Lazarus could see that he was still wearing his usual clothes: black T-shirt, black jeans. So why the disguise? Why would he dress like this?

Lazarus spat and felt his snapped tooth slice across his lips, leaving a trail of red spit to dribble down his cheek, and a moment later heard it land with a dull chink on the ground. He looked over to see it sitting in the dirt on the ground like a piece of broken moonlight. He blinked, couldn't find it again, eyes blurry with tears and pain, out of focus.

As he tried to pull himself together, images suddenly blasted Lazarus's brain like a lightning storm, blowing it into a thousand bloody pieces. Everything came at him at once and he gripped his head, winced in pain, half expected bits of skull to burst out like streamers in a party popper.

Nausea swept over him like a tidal wave, only instead of hitting him once, it came at him again and again and again like it wanted him to drown in it. Lazarus was overwhelmed. He froze in an attempt to stop himself throwing up, breathed deep.

Don't puke . . . please God don't puke . . .

But that only made things worse. A stench on the air, like rotting flesh, rushed into his nostrils like they were sewer pipes. A metallic taste licked the edges of his tongue. And nature took over.

Stomach emptied, Lazarus slumped.

Blinked.

He was in a cavern, that much he could make out. But something was wrong. It looked horribly – *felt* horribly – familiar.

This was all too much. He felt like death. Perhaps that was it; maybe he was dead . . .

At last the nausea faded a little and Lazarus again chanced a glance at where he was. He found his tooth again, lying just in front of him in the grubby, dirty light. He squinted around, rubbed grit from his pained eyes, squeezed them tight shut, opened them.

Once again Lazarus was struck by how familiar the place looked, even though he'd never been here before. OK, so he liked the dark, but that didn't mean it was normal to find himself lost in a creepy cavern that stank of death.

A sound rippled in the darkness, like a dog slurping water from a bowl. Lazarus turned slowly to see what it was, not sure he really wanted to find out.

A few metres away a body was lying against the wall of the cavern like a discarded doll, the limbs slumped and bent. Whoever this person was, they were lying still and quiet, breathing slowly, covered in dust and rubble like they'd just survived a bomb blast.

Lazarus squinted harder to see who it was, but dust and smoke in the air made it difficult. He rubbed his eyes again, felt water against his hands, grit in his eyes, looked harder.

A shadow was stooping over the body.

Breath caught in his throat. Lazarus couldn't tear his eyes away, and kept staring, drilling his eyes into the thick, oily blackness leaning over the person on the floor. For a moment he thought it was just shadows playing on the rocky wall, but the way it was moving made that impossible. It swayed. Bits of it were tattered and torn; in places he could see the wall of the cavern through it. Something black and oozing was spilling from it, slipping into the mouth of the body on the floor from the thing's own, or at least that's where Lazarus assumed it was coming from; he could see no head.

Lazarus rubbed his eyes again, blinked, stared. And now he recognised the body under the shadow. The crazy red hair was a dead giveaway; only one person he knew would happily wear that much of it on his head and let it grow wild like bramble. It was his best mate, Craig.

Lazarus yelled out.

The shadow snapped up and whipped round on Lazarus. Bits of it seemed to break off and fade as it moved. Lazarus could just make out a face in the darkness, or what was left of one: grey skin stretched so tight that with every movement fresh splits oozed horribly, a nose nothing more than two ragged holes, eyes like stab wounds, and a mouth that grinned teeth and bone and blood. But with that grin, Lazarus saw the thing fall backwards a little, like it didn't know whether to be happy or afraid.

He was on his feet. Fast. And he knew what he was facing, his memory now suddenly filling up like a bucket dropped down a well. This thing was one of the Dead. And it didn't matter how nuts that sounded; Lazarus knew it was the awful, terrible truth.

'You get the hell away from him!'

Something deep down, something *instinctive*, told Lazarus it wanted to take Craig's body for itself. And if he didn't stop it, Craig would have one of the Dead inside him and Lazarus would have no option but to rip it back out by whatever means necessary. Something he then remembered that he'd only ever done twice before. And both times it had almost killed him.

The thing laughed and Lazarus was caught by a sulphurous stench in the air. He coughed, and realised he was gripping something in his left hand. Glancing down, a bloodied sight met him; his hand looked like it had got into a brawl with a bag of nails. He was clasping a metal spike, long and terrible, and his own blood was running freely down it from where he was holding it. Lazarus opened his fingers and saw thin spikes, like thorns, jutting out from the handle, hooked deep into his skin. The gory sight made him yell. He tried to let go but he couldn't shake it free. Yet despite the blood, Lazarus felt no pain. The spike was a part of him, he realised. So he closed his hand again, squeezing it white-knuckle tight.

Lazarus's mind suddenly cleared like fog burned away by the sun. He didn't just know where he was, but why. This was the land of the Dead and he was here to find his father.

The thing hissed, cocked its head to one side. 'You are supposed to be dead, boy!'

'Tell me something I don't know,' Lazarus muttered to himself, wondering briefly how the creature knew of him, a little freaked out.

Lazarus moved towards the thing, watching it sway left, right, left. It looked like it was a memory of what a human had once been, its limbs stretched like soft toffee pulled till it almost breaks. And each limb seemed to have far too many joints, bending in directions that made no sense at all.

The thing fell back again, but scuttled back to Craig like it couldn't let him go.

'You can't have him. He's mine!'

It was a wet voice, filled with phlegm and fluid and venom, and it spat from the creature's face like fat from a hot pan. But Lazarus wasn't listening. He gripped the spike harder, felt something break the skin of the back of his hand. When he glanced down, he saw the points of thorns poking through. Were they growing? Something else that didn't make sense. And where was the pain? Why didn't it hurt?

A glob of black spit landed at his feet and bubbled. Lazarus stepped over it.

'A fresh body, lovely and warm! It will suit me, don't you agree?'

Lazarus took another step closer.

'Or perhaps I'll have you, boy, hmm? You look even more desirable . . . Tasty even.'

A purple-black tongue fell from the thing's mouth, snaked and crawled round its face, then slipped back inside.

Lazarus raised the spike, stared the creature down. It snarled, spat again and leant over Craig, covering his body completely.

'You stay away from him, you freak!' Lazarus yelled as his mind swirled and panic tried to take hold. He was here to find his dad, not watch his best mate get possessed.

Sweat beaded, dripped and fell.

But I've got no back-up . . . It's just me . . .

A single, bone-white finger was pointing at him.

'I think I'll have you both,' said the creature.

2
☠☠☠ BLOODY HANDS ☠☠☠

Out of nowhere, a wind hushed round Lazarus and his feet started to slide from under him, like a truck had charged past him on a road, sucking the air along with it.

The creature's face was cracked by a smile that looked like an axe wound. Where its finger had been, there was now a swirling hole of flesh and bone, spinning violently like meat in a blender. And it was growing, consuming the creature from finger to hand to wrist, slowly moving up the arm. The sound of it was horrific, a wet crunching squelch that echoed round the cavern.

The wind sucking Lazarus forward was growing stronger. He dropped to the floor, tried to grab on to something to stop himself sliding closer to the thing bent over Craig. But everything he held just crumbled or pulled away. The rocky ground clawed at his body as he was dragged backwards, the clothes he was wearing tearing easily. He rolled over, tried to use the spike as an anchor, but it just slid through the rock, scratching and carving a deep gouge across the floor.

A sickening snap and crunch of bone made Lazarus look up and he saw the creature's arm, or what was left of it, finally give way. The swirling hole was now large enough to swallow him completely, and at its centre all he could see was darkness. But the hole was still growing. Now Lazarus could see bits of the creature falling into the horrible whirlpool, tearing away in great fleshy strips. All the while, that awful grin stayed on its face, its screams a mix of pain and excitement.

The creature howled, and as if obeying it, the wind tugged even harder at Lazarus, dragging him across the floor, closer and closer to the hole.

Lazarus sucked in air and yelled, 'Craig!'

Nothing.

'Craig! Wake up! Bloody well wake up and do something!'

Craig stirred. Lazarus was sure of it. He shouted again

to make sure. And this time Craig didn't just stir. He coughed and spluttered and arched his back, then spat black fluid across the floor like a tyre mark on a road.

Lazarus saw terror do its best to crush Craig's face as he looked at the creature, then at Lazarus. Craig tried to back away in panic, but was up against the cavern wall.

'Lazarus! What the . . . Lazarus! Help me!'

Lazarus pointed at the creature swaying over Craig. 'We have to stop whatever it's doing!' he shouted.

But he knew Craig wasn't listening. He was scrabbling along the cavern wall, inching away.

'What is it, Laz? What the hell is it! Where are we? What's going on?'

Craig was too terrified to remember what had brought them to this place. Fear had wiped his mind of all but what was happening right here, right now.

'I'll explain later!' Lazarus called. 'You've just got to trust me! We need to . . .'

But his voice was snatched away as the wind tugged again. He tried again with the spike, leant all his weight on it. It slowed him down a little, but it wasn't enough, not in the slightest.

Lazarus saw a spark of recollection in Craig's eyes; it was coming back to him.

'Laz! The spike!' he cried.

Craig was sitting up now, his face grey with dust and streaked with blood. He looked like a corpse, but his eyes were alive and wild with fear.

'The spike, Laz!' yelled Craig again, beckoning with his hands. 'Chuck it to me – now!'

Laz was only a few metres away and with a snap of his arm hurled the spike over to Craig. It sped through the air to land at his friend's feet.

Comprehension shattered the creature's face when it saw what Craig was now holding. It opened its mouth, reached down with its remaining arm . . .

But was too late.

Craig grabbed the spike with both hands, threw his body behind it, and drove it home. It sunk in like a pin into jelly.

The wind stopped in an instant, the spike rammed up to the hilt in the creature's belly. Craig was still holding on, his blood running freely from the wounds on his hands caused by the thorns on the spike's handle. As if the pain only then bit home, Craig let go of the handle with a shocked yelp and scuttled across the floor, away from the creature and towards Lazarus.

'You OK?' asked Lazarus, his body heaving with short, sharp breaths, his eyes still on the startled creature.

Craig nodded, stared at his hands. 'This kills though,' he said. 'What's going on, Laz? What is that thing? I can remember bits, but it's more like a nightmare.'

'Not a bad comparison,' said Lazarus, looking at Craig's bloody hands.

A faint whine buzzed into the cavern. The creature was silent now. The whirling vortex that had been sucking Lazarus in was no more. Instead, that whole side of the creature was unrecognisable. What was left simply hung there, bits of flesh and bone like blood-wet strips of cloth caught on a fence.

The whine stopped. The creature's face winced. Then, with an almost inaudible 'pop', it burst. Rags and flesh and bone rained down like confetti.

Silence.

Neither Lazarus nor Craig spoke, the only sound was that of their breathing. If Lazarus was honest, he didn't really know what to say anyway. Nothing in his head could even begin to describe what he'd just seen.

'Where are we?' asked Craig, breaking the quiet at last. 'What happened?'

Lazarus wiped his forehead with his sleeve. He wasn't about to short circuit Craig's brain with the truth. Not quite yet; give him a few moments to recover. 'How are your hands?' he asked.

Despite the blood still wet and slick on his skin, Craig's palms were relatively undamaged. A few punctures were visible, but none were very deep and most had already stopped bleeding. Compared to the ones Lazarus had in his own hands, they were more like pin pricks.

'I thought it'd be worse than that,' said Craig, squeezing his hand shut and opening it again, testing it, unconvinced that it shouldn't hurt a lot more than it did. 'It stung like hell when I realised what I'd done.'

'If you hadn't woken up,' said Lazarus, 'that thing . . . it would've had us.'

'So we were lucky, then?'

'Could say that.'

Craig spat. 'God, my mouth tastes like a sewer.'

Lazarus remembered the thing dripping black fluid into Craig and decided to say nothing. No one really wants to know that one of the Dead spewed up into their mouth. Sometimes, the truth was best kept hidden.

'I'm afraid I didn't bring any chewing gum,' said Lazarus.

'Then you'll just have to turn your head away when I'm speaking.'

Lazarus smiled. Craig had an unshakable talent at making light of even the darkest of moments.

After everything that had just happened, the cavern felt oddly calm. Lazarus was pleased. It was giving him a few moments to get his head together.

'You saved us both,' he said, unable to stop himself sounding momentarily serious. 'I wouldn't have stood a chance. And if it had got me, you'd have been next.'

'You can buy me a drink when we get back,' replied Craig. 'Which is what we're going to do now, right? Get back?'

Lazarus went to say something about going to find his dad, but Craig winced suddenly and grabbed his head like he was afraid it was about to explode.

'Craig? What's wrong?'

Lazarus was worried. The pain he'd just seen splinter Craig's face reminded him of what he'd felt when he'd woken up a few minutes ago.

'Headache,' Craig said, relaxing after a moment. 'Felt like my eyes were about to burst. It's gone now.'

'Sure?'

'Totally.' Craig pushed himself to his feet to look around. 'So what was that thing? How come we're in this cavern? And what's with that car wreck over there?'

'You don't remember, do you?'

Craig shook his head, flexed his damaged hand. 'Not much. Like I said, it's more like a nightmare . . .'

'You sure that's not just because you watch all those horror movies?'

'Well aren't you the comedian,' said Craig.

'No, not really,' Lazarus replied.

'If you're not careful, you'll kill me with your mirth. Seriously.'

Lazarus nodded slowly. 'What *do* you remember?'

Craig looked thoughtful for a minute, then said, 'Well, I know this place is under your house and that we came down here looking for something . . . Yeah, that was it: a clue to finding your dad, right?'

Lazarus nodded again.

'What about this cavern? What do you remember about what happened . . . here?'

Craig shook his head. 'I know I'm going to regret asking this, Laz, but why don't you just tell me? It'll be quicker.'

Lazarus sighed. 'You sure? It's going to sound crazy.'

'I like crazy.'

Lazarus composed himself. 'A few nights ago, a creature calling itself Red appeared in my house to tell me to get a message to my dad. To tell him that the Dead are coming.'

Craig opened his mouth to say something but shut it quickly. His wide-eyed look of confusion said more than enough.

'Since then,' continued Lazarus, trying to keep it short, 'I've been killed and resurrected by an angel, attacked by your friend Clair who had one of the Dead inside her, and discovered that as my dad has disappeared off into the land of the Dead to find my long-dead mum, it's my job to take over the family business. Namely being the new Keeper.'

'Keeper?' said Craig, struggling to keep up. 'I thought your dad was into security and collected clocks?'

'There's a lot we thought about my dad,' said Lazarus, unable to hide the hurt and confusion in his voice. 'None of it true. Turns out he's spent his life keeping the Dead where they belong. And now it's my turn.'

Lazarus could almost see Craig processing the information he'd just been given.

'So that Dead thing that just attacked us,' said Craig at last. 'If it's from the land of the Dead, then how did it get here? What the crap was it doing under your house?'

Lazarus took a deep, deep breath.

'You're not supposed to be here,' he said. 'To be honest, neither of us are. But when Legion threw you through the veil, I had no choice.'

'Legion? Veil? What are you talking about?'

Lazarus took a deep breath. 'Believe it or not, mate,' he said, 'we're not under my house any more . . . We're in the land of the Dead.'

3

CORPSE CLOTHES

'You're shitting me.'

Lazarus shook his head, though he knew just how nuts it all sounded. 'It's the truth. We were in the cavern with Arielle. This thing calling itself Legion came through the veil and—'

'That name rings a bell,' said Craig. 'Wings come in to it somewhere . . .'

'She's the one who shot me. She's an angel.'

'That explains the wings. What about the veil?'

Lazarus pointed over to the car wreck in the middle of the cavern. 'See how it looks weird, like it's under water or something?'

Craig nodded slowly, deliberately, like he was trying to let everything sink into his brain just one insane point at a time.

'That's the veil,' said Lazarus. 'It's the barrier between the Living and the Dead. It's what Clair opened a rip in back at my house. And if you think that sounds crazy, none of this gets any better. There's another veil too, between the Dead and Hell. You remembering any of this yet?'

Lazarus was concerned. Craig must've really cracked his head to whack all of this out of his memory. Maybe it had something to do with that creature that they'd just destroyed. He hoped Craig's memory returned soon. Lazarus didn't want to spend ages going over what he was already trying very hard to forget.

Craig was quiet, thoughtful. Then he looked at Lazarus, rubbed his head and said, 'Actually, yes, I am. I think I was still in a daze from whatever happened to me. But now . . .'

'You remember, right?'

The look on Craig's face said enough. 'Hell's teeth, Laz, I remember all of it.'

For the next few minutes, they went over everything that had happened. Craig was both horrified and excited by it all, whereas Lazarus just wanted to make sure his friend was fine.

'So let me get this absolutely straight,' said Craig at last, 'because I need to know this is what happened so I don't think I'm going nuts . . .'

Lazarus waited for Craig to continue speaking.

'A bloke with no skin turned up at your house, told you to tell your dad that the Dead were coming and he needed to do something about it.'

Lazarus nodded. It was hard not to laugh. Listening to Craig talk in such a matter-of-fact way made it all sound like an everyday occurrence. And it really, seriously wasn't.

'We got Clair round from that paranormal investigating group that I know and it all went pear-shaped.'

Again Lazarus nodded, though pear-shaped was a bit of an understatement.

'Then Arielle the angel turns up, kills and resurrects you, then we go on some nut-job hunt for your missing dad and end up in this weird cavern hidden under your house battling with the Dead.'

'That's about it,' said Lazarus.

'There's just one thing I don't understand.'

'And what's that?'

Craig paused, then said, 'Everything.'

Lazarus at last allowed himself to smile.

'So what do we do now?'

It was a fair question, thought Lazarus, but he didn't really want to answer it. Arielle had told him to do one thing, but his heart and mind, his whole being, was set on something else entirely.

'I think Dad's in trouble,' he said. 'And I'm the only person who can help him. I need his help too; Arielle told me to close the hole in the veil we just came through, but I haven't a clue how.'

'You should study more.'

Lazarus looked up at Craig. 'Look, you should go back. Through the veil. Arielle's on the other side. But I've got to go find Dad.'

'On your own? Here? You're joking, right?'

'What else do you expect me to do?' Lazarus couldn't help snapping. He was making this up as he went along and it was getting more and more difficult. 'I can't just leave him here, can I?'

'That's not what I meant,' answered Craig. 'But

you've got to admit it's crazy. If we are where you say we are, what chance have you got?'

'Dad's gone after Mum,' said Lazarus. 'He thinks he can bring her back or something. But if he doesn't come back soon, then the hole in the veil will get bigger and bigger and the Dead will flood through. I've not got any choice!'

'So we're just going to walk through the land of the Dead asking if anyone's seen your dad, is that it? You don't think we'll stand out a little, being as we're alive?'

'What's with the we?' Lazarus demanded.

'Where you go, I go.'

Lazarus felt a rush of gratitude towards his friend. He walked away from Craig, back to where he'd landed after coming through the veil, and picked up the spike and the rags of clothes he'd brought with him for his friend.

'Here,' he said, handing Craig the clothes. 'I got these from those coffins we found.'

Craig took the clothes but didn't look happy about it.

'Dad used the clothes of corpses as a sort of disguise or something.'

'I remember,' said Craig, holding the clothes as if they were contaminated with something life-threatening.

'Considering what you usually wear, it'll be an improvement.'

'And that coming from someone who takes his style tips from inside the covers of *Kerrang!*?'

Craig pulled the rags over his clothes. They were fragile and in places split and tore as he put them on. His laughter was hollow and cold as he paraded his new clothes in front of Lazarus. 'You really think if we dress like a corpse the Dead will ignore us? Didn't work very well just now, did it?'

'It's still the best chance we've got,' said Lazarus.

'But aren't we going back first? Don't we need Arielle or something? I mean, your dad could be anywhere. He might not even be here at all. Have you thought about that?'

'He's here,' said Lazarus. 'I know it. I can sense it. And no, don't ask me how.'

Lazarus sank deep into his thoughts for a moment. Craig's voice brought him back to the now.

'How come you're not screaming when you're holding

31

that thing? When I held it I thought my hand had been ripped off.'

Craig was staring at the spike. He was holding it in his left hand and the three-edged blade of the thing was red with Lazarus's blood. He turned it point upwards, then lifted it in front of his face.

When Craig saw Lazarus's hand, his eyes went wide like saucers. 'That's . . . that's just not right! How can you not feel that? I mean those spikes on the handle . . . they go right through your bloody hand! And I mean that literally!'

Lazarus twisted the spike to look at the back of his hand. The thorns from the handle were clearly visible sticking through it, each one razor-sharp. And they were definitely bigger than when Craig had held it, almost as though they were feeding off Lazarus, using his blood to grow. He'd noticed it earlier, when he'd just appeared in the cavern. But seeing them now made it real.

'And all that blood,' said Craig, 'not a drop's hitting the floor. It's like that spike's absorbing it or something.'

Lazarus knew Craig was right; it was sucking up his

blood. When he flipped the spike to point back down towards the ground and stuck the thing under his belt, where the thorns on the handle had pushed through his palm, the holes remained. He could see all the way through to the other side. But there was no pain, no pain at all.

Craig walked over to the car wreck.

'This veil thing,' he said, reaching out to prod it. The surface rippled. 'So you're saying we came through it? And on the other side is a cavern, just like this one, but with Arielle in it?'

'Yeah,' Lazarus answered. 'But I don't get why this place is basically a mirror image of where we came from.'

A small drop of blood fell from Craig's hands towards the veil. When it touched it, for a minute it simply hung there, suspended impossibly in the shimmering surface that covered the wreck. Then it slipped further in and disappeared, a charge of electricity spreading outwards like cracks in ice from the place where it had vanished.

Craig pulled his hand away and looked at Lazarus. 'So how do you shut this down, then?' he asked, gesturing at the veil. 'How do you block up the hole?'

Lazarus said nothing, just stared at the car wreck that had killed his mum; killed him, too. And that was the riddle in all this, wasn't it? He'd been killed twice. Once by accident, then again on purpose. Both times he'd been pulled back. The first time had been by Red, the bloodied creature who'd come looking for his dad. Red had saved Lazarus as an infant, stopped him crossing over to the land of the Dead by pushing him back. The second had been by Arielle after she'd shot him. She'd told him that to be a Keeper, he had to taste death first. But the fact he'd tasted it twice had changed things. He didn't know how or why, but it had.

'Laz?'

Lazarus looked up.

'You OK?' asked Craig. 'You spaced out there for a minute.'

Lazarus forced a smile as he pushed his thoughts deep down. Now was not the time. 'Sorry,' he said. 'It's just a lot to take in, that's all.'

Craig rested a hand on Lazarus's shoulder. 'Then let's get back to Arielle,' he said. 'She's been wrapped up in all of this for ever. She's a part of it, which I guess explains why she drinks so much.'

'She told me not to come,' said Lazarus. 'And I'm not sure taking an angel into the land of the Dead is that sensible, do you?'

'She'll know what to do, though, surely!'

'It's not that simple,' said Lazarus.

He could tell Craig was concerned and that, although he was disguising it well, he wanted to get back. Hardly a surprise. He'd been dragged into this by accident and things had just gone from bad to worse to full-on stinking, rancid mess. Why shouldn't he want to go back home? But Lazarus couldn't do that. Not yet. He had a job to do and his dad was depending on him. And the feelings running through him now were confusing as hell. A few days ago he'd have happily walked away from his dad and never seen him again. But now, after everything he'd found out, things had changed. He wanted his dad back. And there was no moving him on this, no moving at all.

'We need her, Laz,' said Craig. 'We go on from here alone, we're going to end up dead. Or worse.'

When Lazarus next spoke, his voice was little more

than a whisper. 'Dad was supposed to tell me,' he said, staring into the middle distance. 'Train me up, show me what to do. But he's not here. And I'm not ready.'

'What are you talking about?'

Lazarus whipped round. 'I'm not ready for this!' Even he was surprised by the anger in his voice. 'I don't know how to close the damned hole! I don't know how to do any of this!'

'Then let's ask Arielle.'

'Arielle doesn't know either,' Lazarus snapped. 'She's the Keeper's guardian angel. It's not her job to do stuff like this. She doesn't know any more than I do!'

Lazarus stopped speaking.

'The only one who knows enough to help us,' he said, his voice a little calmer, 'is Dad. He came this way before us. The only chance we have is if we find him. He must know how to close the hole or he wouldn't have opened it in the first place.'

'But we don't know where he is!' said Craig, unable to hide his frustration. 'And not only that, we don't even know where we are either, so we're totally screwed whichever way you look at it!'

But Lazarus wasn't listening. He'd spotted something in the far wall of the cavern that had got him thinking.

'Steps,' he said, pointing across the cavern. 'Over there. Just like the ones we came down into the cavern on the other side of the veil.'

'So?'

'So,' said Lazarus, 'what if this place is actually exactly the same as where we've come from?'

'I was with you up to *what if*,' said Craig. 'Then you lost me.'

Lazarus didn't wait to explain. He dashed across to the steps. He turned back to Craig. 'You ready to use all that research you've done on horror movies and act like you're dead?'

'You're not making any sense!' Craig cried. 'Have you heard yourself? We need to go back through this veil thing, get out of here! We can't head right into the land of the Dead! What if more of those creatures come? Then what?'

'I have to find my dad, Craig,' said Lazarus, and nothing or no one was going to change his mind.

'I can't leave him here.'

'But you don't even like him!' said Craig, exasperated. 'You hardly even know him!'

'Exactly!' Lazarus shouted back. 'That's why I'm here! Don't you get it? He's the only dad I've got. The only relative. Without him, it's just me. I need to find him!'

For a second or two, the boys stared at each other across the stillness of the cavern. Between them, the veil shimmered over the wrecked car. Then Lazarus nodded, turned, and disappeared up the steps. Craig was his best friend, but nothing was going to change his mind now; he was going to find his dad and that was that.

At the top of the steps was another cavern. Lazarus saw more steps rising up ahead. If his hunch was right, then at the top of those he'd find something utterly impossible: a cellar, and a house.

He started to move towards them when a scuffle made him snap round.

'You're absolutely bloody mental,' said Craig, emerging from the top of the steps Lazarus had just run up. 'It's one of the qualities that keeps me interested in still being your friend. Well, that and the fact that I need to educate you properly in horror movies.'

Lazarus smiled. 'The clothes suit you,' he said. 'For the first time in your life you look almost presentable.'

Craig walked over, looked at the steps ahead. 'So we go up there then, yeah?'

Lazarus nodded.

And they both stepped into the darkness.

4
☠ SAVAGED FACE ☠

'Déjà vu,' said Craig as he followed Lazarus off the top step and into the room beyond. 'But a little bit more creepy.'

Lazarus said nothing, just shuffled forward, stopped.

The room was small, dark, and looked like a grenade had turned up with a bunch of its mates and had a good time. No matter where Lazarus stared, he couldn't find anything that wasn't in some way damaged. The table, which had obviously once stood in the centre of the room, was now nothing but a crumbling pile of firewood. The work benches, and the shelves along the walls, were all falling apart, smashed, ruined. And in a dusty corner, a crippled wine rack leant uselessly against the wall, looking down mournfully on a mound of sour-smelling broken bottles. On the other side of the room the broken remains of a door hung on its hinges like a drunk trying to stop itself falling to the ground. Lazarus knew that more steps led upwards beyond the door. And he had a gut feeling that he knew what lay beyond them as well.

'Is this actually real?' asked Craig as Lazarus looked around where he was now standing. 'OK, so I know it's real, because I'm here and I can see it and touch it, but it's not possible! It can't be! I mean this is . . .'

'I know,' said Lazarus, taking over where Craig's voice disappeared. And then he spoke the reality of where they were, trying to convince himself that to hear his own voice say it would make it OK. 'It's Dad's workshop. The one under our house.'

Trouble was, saying it out loud didn't help it make any more sense.

'Except this isn't that workshop, is it?' said Craig. 'Because, if I'm to believe everything you've said, we're in the land of the Dead, right?'

He picked up an old mug that was missing its handle. It crumbled in his hands. 'This is like a nightmare version of the real world,' he said, dusting his fingers. 'And just so you know, nothing you can say will make me feel any better about all this, you know that, don't you?'

Lazarus picked his way across the floor. He was careful not to trip, but stopped when he heard something crunch underfoot. He looked down to see his right foot resting in the broken glass of a tattered picture frame.

'What is it?' asked Craig, not moving from where he was stood.

Lazarus shifted his foot, crouched down. Under the broken glass and rubble, he could just about see the back of a photograph. Carefully he pulled it free, shook it clean, then stood up. But when he flipped it over the image he saw hit him with such force he nearly fell backwards.

The photograph fell from Lazarus's hands. He steadied himself against the wall, saw the memories of his mum go up in flames.

'You've gone white,' said Craig. 'And considering everything you've seen since all this kicked off, that's saying something.'

'It's that photo of Mum,' said Lazarus, his eyes wide and staring as Craig picked up the photograph. 'The one that was on the wall when we were in Dad's workshop. It had that keyhole behind it for this.'

Lazarus reached up to touch the small silver key hanging on a silver chain round his neck. It was probably the only decent birthday present his dad had ever given him. And it had opened a door in the wall of his workshop that had eventually taken them to the car wreck and the veil, and ultimately to where they were now.

'I don't understand,' said Craig. 'If it's just a photograph, what's the problem?'

'Don't look at it,' said Lazarus. 'Seriously . . . Just don't look at it.'

But Craig's interest was already piqued. Lazarus watched his friend flip the photograph up in front of him, then saw his own emotions etched into Craig's eyes like scratches in a mirror.

'I told you not to look,' said Lazarus and held out his hand to take the photograph.

'Laz . . .' Craig's shock was breathless. 'I mean, I've never seen anything like that. Her *eyes* . . .'

Lazarus looked once more at the photograph. Yeah, it was his mum all right. He'd recognise her anywhere; his house was filled with pictures of her. He'd grown up with her ghost a part of his everyday life, thanks to his dad's complete inability to move on from her death all those years ago. But this photo . . . it was *wrong* . . .

Lazarus forced himself to look again. Her face looked like it had been savaged by an animal. The skin hung from it, loose and sore, her mouth frozen in an endless, soundless scream. And stretching from her scalp and down between her eyes, a gash seemed to split her in two, like the skin was pulling away from itself, slipping further and further until it would eventually lose hold and leave nothing but a raw skull and bloody muscle. But it was the eyes that drew him in. They looked terribly alive, like what had happened to her in the photograph was still happening. And, most awful and haunting of all, it looked like she was enjoying it. Or had no choice but to try.

Swallowing hard, Lazarus forced himself to look away, and folded it into four. He tried to stop the tears, but it was a waste of time. Streaks of heat flowed down his cheeks. The enormity and the insanity of what he was doing had just sideswept him like a skull crack from a cricket bat. His family wasn't dysfunctional, it was . . . Well, just what the hell was it? His mum was dead. His dad was insane. If only it were that simple. It wasn't. And seeing the mum he didn't remember, the mum who used to appear in dreams yet fade as the years went by, now appear in a photograph like a special-effects extra in a gory horror movie . . . It was too much. He wanted to run and hide and scream and yell and . . . But nothing would work, he knew that. No act he could carry out would change anything. Except, perhaps, what he was about to do. Yeah, life made no sense. Yeah, if he told anyone normal (Craig really didn't count) what he was going through right now, they'd have him in a straight jacket immediately. But it didn't matter where he was, what had happened or what was about to happen. His dad was out there. And he was the only family he had left, and he was going to get him back. Even if it killed him. Which, Lazarus thought with a slight smile, it already had. So what was there to be afraid of?

Stuffing the photograph into his pocket, and pushing all those insanity-inducing thoughts way way down with it, Lazarus heard Craig shuffle across the floor to join him.

'That bench,' said Craig, looking at the wall of the room. 'Is it me, or does it look like someone's propped it up?'

Lazarus turned to see what Craig was on about. 'How do you mean?'

'Everything else is on the floor,' said Craig, 'but not that bit. And if you look at what's holding it up, the only way that piece of wood could've got there is if someone jammed it in.'

Craig was right. It really did look like someone had braced the bench somehow. His dad?

'And that's one of your dad's clocks, isn't it?' asked Craig, pointing at the small timepiece sitting on the bench. 'How come it's almost in one piece when everything else here is totally smashed up?'

Lazarus didn't answer immediately. He was staring at the dust on the surface of the broken bench. It had been brushed away, he could see that now, and in places he could make out the marks of fingers, a palm print. It could only be his dad. Who else would have been this way and had the skill to put just one of the clocks back together?

'Laz . . .'

Craig's voice was quiet, like it had something to say but didn't want to be heard.

'What?'

'I found these,' he said, and handed what was in his hand over to Lazarus. 'Look like those diaries you read when we were last here. Not that we've been here before. Anyway, you know what I mean.'

Lazarus took them.

'They're the ones your dad wrote about your mum and stuff,' said Craig. 'I didn't mean to look, it's private, I know that. The pages sort of fell open and . . .'

'It's OK,' said Lazarus, looking down at the diaries now in his hands. He remembered them from the other side of the veil, in the land of the Living. What he'd read then had told him things about his dad he was still having trouble dealing with; his love not just for his mum, but for Lazarus himself. And that's why Lazarus was here, wasn't it? It wasn't about the Dead or any of that creepy stuff. No. He was here to get back the father he'd never really known. To have that chance to start over.

'No, it's not,' said Craig. 'Look at the pages. They're not OK at all.'

Lazarus picked out one of the diaries, placed the others by the clock, then opened it. It pretty much opened itself.

The words were utterly illegible. The pages of the diary were scorched and scratched and stained in blood, the words nothing but blotches and scars. Lazarus could just about make out that it was his dad's writing – the occasional swoop of a 'y' or 'g', or every now and again a letter standing stark and alone among its ruined cousins – but not one word could be read.

'This is getting really freaky,' said Craig as Lazarus closed the diary, placed it back with the others. 'I mean, I'm not sure it can be anything else *but* freaky, but seriously – what the hell's going on?'

Lazarus said nothing. He wasn't sure how long ago, but he knew his dad had been here. He'd sensed it from the moment he'd stepped through the veil, but now, seeing the clock, that was confirmation enough. He wasn't turning back now. No chance.

'Laz?' said Craig. 'You still with me? What

are we going to do?'

Lazarus turned to answer, to tell Craig they were going to get his dad, find him and take him home and make everything right again . . . but he didn't get a chance as a thump slammed into the room. Lazarus and Craig dropped to the floor, terror shredding the screams in their throats. The floor shook, bits of the ceiling fell around them and the walls buckled.

'What the hell was that?' hissed Craig.

A distant roar ruptured the air and drilled into them like it was trying to shatter their skulls. It sounded like a thousand voices spitting venom and anger.

Lazarus didn't want to know what it was and decided to ignore it. Whatever it was, it was out there and that, at this very minute, meant nothing to him. All that mattered was the next steps he was going to take, the ones which led him closer to his dad.

Then the dust started to settle, rubble and dust and plaster tumbled down – and the way back down the steps to the veil collapsed in on itself like a pack of cards.

5
☠ BLACK HOLE ☠

'We're trapped,' said Craig, choking on dust.

Lazarus didn't even bother to glance at his friend. He just stood up, brushed himself down and then walked over to where they'd entered the room. The idea that they could dig their way out faded like ice melting in the sun. The space where the doorway had been was now filled with boulders too large for either of them to move. He pulled at one just to make sure. It shifted a little, but all that did was to cause more rocks to tumble down from above. Lazarus jumped out of the way just in time as the rubble crashed around him.

'Nice try,' said Craig, pushing himself on to his knees then to his feet. 'Don't suppose you've got a stick of dynamite or two, have you?'

Lazarus shook his head, couldn't stop a faint smile.

Craig was indomitable.

'Worth a stab,' said Craig. 'So now what?'

'Don't think we've got any choice,' Lazarus said, nodding towards the broken door at the other end of the workshop and making his way across the floor. 'Only one person can help us now, and that's Dad.' He paused, shook his head. 'Can't say this is exactly going according to plan.'

'You mean you had a plan?'

'No,' said Lazarus. 'Is it that obvious?'

Lazarus wondered if Craig knew just how dreadful, scary almost, he now looked. His face was still streaked with dried blood, dust all over him. The looking-like-a-corpse disguise was working better than he could've ever imagined.

'So,' said Craig, 'I don't suppose you've got any idea where your dad might be, have you? Or how we're going to find him?'

'Not really,' said Lazarus, thinking. 'But if what we've seen so far is anything to go by, then this place – well, it's like the land of the Living, just . . . dead, I guess.'

'How do you mean?'

'This is Dad's workshop,' said Lazarus. 'So I'm guessing that means some version of our house, perhaps even the world beyond, is above us. If we can get up into the rest of the house, then we might find a few more clues. Dad's study must be up there so he might have gone there too.'

'Then we'd better go find out,' said Craig and clambered over what was left of the workshop to Lazarus. 'No point waiting around, is there?'

As he was nearing Lazarus, Craig stopped, stooped down to the floor. 'I thought you put this in your pocket,' he said, picking something up. 'Must've fallen out when the way back to the cavern collapsed.'

'It did,' Lazarus said, reaching out to take the picture Craig was handing to him. 'It's still in my pocket.'

To make sure, he checked, and there it was.

'Must be another one then,' said Craig.

Lazarus opened the folded photograph. He was expecting to see his mum staring back. Instead, he saw himself.

It wasn't exactly new. In the photo he looked no older than ten or eleven. He was in the garden, playing with some toy cars on his own. The photograph had been taken from inside the house, the edge of the kitchen window just visible in the picture.

He couldn't remember the last time his dad had taken a photograph of him. Family days out weren't something that had happened ever, and holidays were something other kids went on. Lazarus wondered if there were others like this. Had his dad been secretly taking pictures of him throughout his life?

'That's you, isn't it?' asked Craig, looking over at the picture. 'You OK?'

Lazarus nodded. 'Dad must've taken it. But why's it here?'

'Well it's not like that one of your mum, is it?'

Craig had a point. This was just a photograph, the kind you'd find at home flashing by on a digital photo frame. Not all warped and ruined and messed up with a chainsaw. A thought struck Lazarus bullet hard. Dad had come here alone, yet with him he'd had a picture of his son. A reminder of normality? Or a hook back to the one thing that meant something to him? Lazarus didn't know. And at that minute he suddenly felt enraged.

Years and years and his dad had never shown him anything except cold acceptance. Yet now, without warning, he was learning that his dad actually loved him and was so much more than he'd ever realised. He had just been protecting Lazarus from the horrifying truth of his – their – life.

Dad was never interested in me,' said Lazarus, and knew he sounded cold. 'And if he was, he certainly never showed it! So why the hell is this here? Actually, why the hell am I here, Craig? What the crap am I doing?'

'When we find him, you can ask him,' Craig said. 'Let's get moving.'

Lazarus's emotions were twisting his gut. Every step he took brought with it something new he'd never known about his dad. Jamming the photograph into his pocket alongside the one of his mum, he pulled open the door to the cellar steps. The handle was rusted, and as the door swung open, bits of wood fell to the floor.

Craig came over and looked at what was left of the steps behind the door. 'Reckon they'll hold us?' he asked.

'They'll have to,' Lazarus answered.

The stairs were twisted and broken, like some force

had tried to turn them into a corkscrew and given up halfway. The door at the top was smashed in, and what was left of it leant away at an impossible angle, occasionally flapping open to show only darkness beyond.

Lazarus's foot went straight through the first step with the crunch of brittle wood.

'Bad sign,' said Craig.

When Lazarus moved again, he braced his hands on the walls leading up the sides of the stairs. Then he placed his feet right at the far edge of each step, thinking that at least there was a chance they'd be stronger where they were fixed. The steps groaned and complained, dust fell, but they held solid.

'Come on,' he said, moving upwards. 'The quicker we get to the top, the better.'

Craig's answer was to follow Lazarus's lead and do exactly as he had. Soon they were in a rhythm, each moving a hand or a foot at exactly the same time, neither speaking. At the top. Lazarus hurled himself through the door on to the floor beyond. It took a few seconds for his eyes to adjust to the darkness. When they did, the reality of the nightmare cemented itself firmly in his mind. This place really was an exact copy of the house he'd grown up in. But here it was as though it was in a constant state of total decay. Like it was always falling apart in some way, but never actually able to completely fall in on itself.

'A hand up would be good,' said Craig from behind him.

Lazarus turned to help. As he reached out the house shook again. Behind Craig, the stairs started to collapse in on themselves, one by one, a great black hole to nowhere opening up underneath them.

Lazarus grabbed Craig's hand, then with the other pulled at his clothes. He gave a heave.

Craig yelled out as the stair he was standing on was sucked to nothing.

'Hold on!' shouted Lazarus, gripping his friend with all his strength.

'I can't!' Craig shouted back. 'There's nothing for my feet to grip on to! It's just a bloody great hole!'

Lazarus pulled harder, felt Craig slip back, pulled again. This time, Craig budged.

'Laz!' shouted Craig. 'LAZ!'

Lazarus closed his eyes and with everything he had, gave a final heave. And Craig came up from the stairs like a cork from a bottle, landing on top of him, then rolling off and away from the stairs that were no longer there.

Silence. Then Craig spoke.

'Not exactly welcoming, is it?'

Lazarus sat up. 'Seems pretty keen to kill us.'

Craig coughed and looked around. 'You were right – this is definitely your house. But it looks like it was hit by an earthquake. And it's dark. I mean, not like the lights are out and it's night outside; like the darkness is actually something you could reach out and touch.'

Lazarus recognised exactly where they were. If he went one way he'd be in the dining room, then through to the kitchen. If he went the other, then he'd be down the hall towards the lounge. It really was freaky. And Craig was right. It was dark. It seemed to glow with a black light, like the shadows of the place were the only thing giving it any depth or substance.

'You OK?'

Craig coughed again and nodded. 'I'm trying not to think about what would've happened to me if you'd not pulled me up. I've a feeling it would've been bad. And painful.'

'This is all bad,' said Lazarus. 'Every bit of it. What we're doing, where we are.'

He felt overwhelmed. Going after his dad was his decision. Craig had ended up being a part of it by accident more than anything. Lazarus didn't want to think about what would have happened if he'd been unable to pull his best friend up either. He wanted to wake from the nightmare he was now walking in. But that wasn't about to happen.

'Let's find your dad and get out of here,' said Craig, standing up. 'Where do you reckon we should start?'

'We go that way, down the hall,' said Lazarus. 'Start with the lounge, then Dad's study.'

'At least the floor looks OK,' Craig said.

'We'll just have to be careful,' warned Lazarus. 'It's like this place knows we're here and wants to get rid of us.'

'Or trap us,' said Craig. 'You ever seen *The Amityville Horror*?'

Lazarus had seen both versions. He'd been freaked out for days afterwards. 'Thanks for the happy thoughts.

You're like a walking hug, you know that?'

He pulled the spike from his belt. The thorns on the handle slipped easily through the holes in his hand. Craig was staring at Lazarus's hand.

'That's almost enough to make me want to puke.'

'Then try not to look,' said Lazarus. 'Come on.'

The carpet in the hall was rotten and lay in pieces, but the floorboards underneath seemed strong enough to hold them. With each step they creaked and groaned, but then Lazarus didn't quite know if it was the boards themselves or the actual house, like the whole place was pissed off that they were there at all and wanted them out pronto. The further they walked the less welcome he felt, like the place was either closing in around them or trying to work out what to do next, how to catch them, how to kill them . . .

'Let's try the lounge,' said Lazarus as they reached the end of the hall at the bottom of the stairs.

Pushing the door open, the memory of what had happened there only days ago came at him like he'd stepped off the pavement and, just too late, seen the truck about to crunch him into the tarmac. It all sounded crazy.

Felt worse. And that was when this had all begun. Would it ever come to an end? Being here made him want to grab time and twist it hard, wrench it back to before all this had turned up to rip his world apart. But he couldn't. Lazarus wasn't sure which pissed him off more; that he could start over, or that he was here in the first place. Either way, he was getting to the point where whatever was about to happen was edging him into a constant state of angry-as-hell. He could feel it in the ends of his fingers, prickly and hot. Somehow, some way, this was going to end badly. He knew it in his gut. But that didn't stop him walking forward.

Lazarus stepped into the gloomy space on the other side of the door, Craig on his heels. The room was empty. The walls were crumbling. Something that looked a little like the sofa from Lazarus's proper house was pushed up against the fire. The mantelpiece mirror was in pieces on the hearth. As for the rest of the furniture in the room, there wasn't much left of it. The walls were crumbling and through the broken windows all Lazarus could make out was yet more darkness.

But that wasn't what bothered him. It was the fact

that the windows were bricked up. This wasn't a house, nor even the reflection of one. This was a sick prison; a twisted version of what you'd had when you were alive, reminding you that you'd never have it again.

'Ignoring the weirdness of the bricked-up windows,' said Craig, 'this room doesn't actually look much different, does it?'

Lazarus went to reply, but something made him turn towards the lounge door.

'What's up?'

'It's that smell again,' said Lazarus, now able to control his response to it, to stop the nausea overcoming him completely. 'Something is here with us. Something dead.'

6
STAINED AND TORN

'Can't you be a bit more specific?'

Lazarus shook his head. So little of what was happening made sense. The fact he was making it up as he went along didn't make him feel any better.

'I can smell it,' he said. At least that was the truth. 'This whole place reeks of death, but there's something else there, too. I just don't know what.'

'In the house?'

Lazarus shrugged. 'Don't know, but it's stronger than when I saw that thing with you in the cavern. He gave the room a final sweeping glance. 'Let's check the rest of the house. Dad might have gone upstairs.'

'Why would he do that?'

Lazarus didn't know – it was all guesswork. 'This is a dead version of our house, isn't it? Maybe he figured when he got here Mum would be here too.'

Back in the hall, Lazarus could see the doorway to his dad's study ahead. To his right the stairs swept grey and broken to the floor above. The large window staring down from the landing halfway up was nothing but a bricked-up hole to whatever lay outside. Lazarus didn't want to find out what that was unless he had to.

'Can you still smell it?' asked Craig.

Lazarus nodded. 'It's not getting any stronger though.'

'Which means whatever's making it isn't getting any closer.'

That's what had happened before anyway, so he'd learnt something at least.

'Where's it coming from?'

'No idea,' said Lazarus. 'We'll get a better idea as we check out the rest of the house.'

'Let's just hope we don't walk in on whatever it is,' said Craig. 'Upstairs, right?'

Lazarus walked to the staircase. 'May as well start at the top and work down.' He stuck close to the wall rather than using the banisters, as what was left of them seemed to be standing more by luck than anything else. Craig followed close behind. The house was silent. Lazarus could hear only the sound of them both breathing.

'Dad's bedroom,' said Lazarus, nodding into the room at the top of the stairs and immediately on their left.

Craig peered in. 'If it's all the same with you, I'll take an upgrade.'

Craig was doing what he did best: making fun of a crappy situation. But he had a point. The bedroom was dust and ash and decay, the bed collapsed, the mattress stained and torn. A wardrobe had fallen across the bed like it had collapsed after a few too many beers. At home, Lazarus could remember how his dad's bedroom was decorated with photographs of his mum. Here the walls were utterly bare, the wallpaper peeling, and brown stains flowered and bloomed everywhere.

Lazarus moved away from the room, turned right.

'Your room?' said Craig, following on behind.

'Yeah,' said Lazarus, keeping to himself the fact that each footstep felt like he was slopping through treacle. 'Dad's no reason to go into it. I just want to see what this place has done to it.'

'Sure that's sensible?'

Lazarus, keeping his reasons to himself, just kept walking until he came to a door.

He pushed it open.

Like the rest of the house, the room was upside down, hacked apart, the windows bricked up. He recognised bits of it: torn versions of his posters hanging dead on the wall, the occasional smashed CD. But as he stepped further inside, he noticed something was different.

The bedcovers had been smoothed out in some attempt to neaten it up. The desk had been dusted down, the chair righted.

'Someone's been here,' said Craig as Laz stopped at the side of the bed. 'Who'd do this, Laz? Why tidy up in here? What's the point?'

Lazarus couldn't work it out. It was like the place had been made ready for him. But no one knew about him being here other than Craig and Arielle. He wondered what Arielle was doing now that he and Craig were in the land of the Dead. She'd warned him not to go. He was beginning to think listening to her might have been a good idea. But he'd had no choice – not with his dad and Craig being in trouble.

'Dad must've done it,' said Lazarus at last. 'Perhaps he felt he was making amends. You know, doing this here somehow meant he'd start doing more at home with me if his plan worked out.'

'You don't sound convinced.'

'I don't sound anything,' said Lazarus. 'But this had to be Dad.'

'What if it was your mum?'

Lazarus hadn't thought about that.

'We don't even know she's here,' he said. 'No, this was Dad. I think he was just trying to make sense of all this Keeper stuff himself.'

'You reckon?'

'Sometimes,' said Lazarus, remembering the rare occasions he would see his dad around the house, 'I'd find him tidying up at home, and he'd be talking and mumbling to himself. It was like doing the job helped him think.'

'Still weird though.'

'That's Dad; weird was his business,' said Lazarus. 'Come on, let's check the study.'

'Then what?'

'If there's nothing there to give us a clue as to where he's gone . . .'

Lazarus's voice faded. He didn't have an answer. He was winging this.

'Then let's just hope we find something,' said Craig.

The study door, like the rest of the doors in the house, was a battered thing only moments away from collapsing. Lazarus reached out and gave it a push. It didn't budge. He went at it with his shoulder. Still nothing. He slid the spike back into his belt and tried again.

'Let me give you a hand,' said Craig, and leaned against the door.

It resisted, then, with a weak sigh, collapsed inwards. Craig and Lazarus toppled forward into the room to land on the floor on what was left of the door.

Lazarus rolled over, sat up, and looked around the room.

'Well at least we know how to make an entrance,'

said Craig from the floor.

'You OK?'

'Nothing broken,' said Lazarus and got to his feet.

Lazarus knew in an instant that his dad had been here. All the furniture was the right way up. The floor had been brushed clear of dust and rubbish. Books were back on shelves, and in some places served to keep the shelves up. The large desk that dominated the room had been swept clean and a broken leg replaced with three or four large books to keep it propped up and level. On top of it, in nice neat piles, were notebooks and papers. Lazarus walked round to the other side of the desk and sat down on the chair pushed under it. Dad had been here, it was obvious – and he'd been unable to stop himself making the room in some way like his true study. Then he must've sorted through the piles of notebooks and papers now on his desk. But why? Lazarus hadn't a clue.

He pulled the first pile of papers towards him and stared at them for a moment.

'What have you found?' asked Craig, perching himself on the other side of the desk.

'Dad's notes,' said Lazarus. 'But they don't make sense – look.'

He handed a few pages to Craig from the top of the pile.

'What's wrong with them? It's your dad's handwriting.'

'Exactly,' said Lazarus. 'These notes haven't been damaged. Remember those diaries you found in the workshop? They were ruined and scratched out. These haven't been touched. '

'What are you saying?'

Lazarus sat back in his chair. It didn't help shuffle his thoughts into any better sense of order.

'I think Dad brought these with him to help him find Mum.'

'So why's he left them here?' asked Craig.

'Because he's coming back,' said Lazarus. 'He knows this place. It's his house, or something like it. That's why he's tidied up in here. We could wait for him. But we've no idea how long that'd take. We just need to work out where he's gone.'

'By reading through this stuff?'

Lazarus knew it sounded crazy, impossible even, but it wasn't like they had any choice.

'It's all I can think of.'

Lazarus knew the frustration in his voice was singing loud and clear. He jabbed a finger hard on the notes like he was trying to staple them together with his bones.

'Dad's been here. He brought this stuff with him for a reason – and that has to be to do with finding Mum. It's not much, but it's all we've got. And unless we find him, we could end up being here for much longer than either of us want.'

'I don't like the sound of that,' said Craig.

'Neither do I,' said Lazarus.

He reached up to the pile of notes to start searching for a clue. But as he did so, the smell he'd noticed in the lounge, that had always seemed just on the edge of everything as they'd searched the house, increased with such violent intensity that he yelled out like a man drowning.

Craig dashed round. 'Laz? What's wrong?'

Lazarus was holding his head. He could feel his blood

thumping through his body. It felt like it was trying to split through his skin, turn him into some kind of burst human balloon. He squeezed his eyes hard shut. He could see stars, and his stomach was tying itself into knots.

'It's that smell,' he said, his voice barely a whisper. 'It just got seriously strong.'

'Why?' asked Craig, as Lazarus at last managed to peel open his eyes again.

'What is it?'

Lazarus didn't reply. Because what he saw standing in the shattered doorway to the study was answer enough. He pointed.

Craig turned.

And the figure in the doorway allowed its face to break into an almost smile of teeth and blood.

7
☠ MASK OF BLOOD ☠

'Lazarus!'

Hearing that voice say his name once more turned Lazarus's world on its head. Everything spun out of control, like Lazarus's whole damned world had been thrown on to a rollercoaster and sent on a free ride to Vomit Central. He saw Craig grab his head, pain creasing his face, then drop to the floor on to his knees, his legs collapsing like broken sticks.

He whimpered like an injured dog.

Lazarus looked back at the figure in the doorway. He'd recognised him instantly, had as soon as he'd heard his name. How could he not? This was hardly the kind of person you forgot, even if you wanted to. And Lazarus really, really did. But they, he – it – was scorched into his brain like a white-hot brand.

'Lazarus,' said the figure once more.

'Red . . .'

The figure nodded, stepped forward, and with the little finger of his left hand caught a drop of blood slipping from the corner of his mouth. Craig toppled backwards, banged into the desk, then froze on the floor.

Lazarus remembered Craig having that headache after they'd got rid of the thing in the cavern. Either it had come back at a very bad time, or seeing Red had brought it on. And he really didn't like the sound of that, made him think about his own reaction to the Dead. But he was a Keeper; it was part of the job. Craig shouldn't have been affected at all.

When they had first met, Red had looked like he'd barely survived a car crash or being thrown through a thousand windows. And as Red had told Lazarus about the Dead returning, Lazarus had watched Red's body slowly heal. Now he looked almost human, though that wasn't saying much. Lazarus knew he was staring. Red's face bore skin now, rather than just a mask of blood and muscle and bone, but it was scarred awfully, almost as though, no matter what Red did, he would never be able to fully rid himself of his wounds. Just how deep did they go? The rest of his body was much the same, though in some places the skin either didn't seem to fit right or was missing completely, and blood seeped freely, made Red's pale skin look like raspberry ripple ice cream.

Before Lazarus could react further, Red was across the room and had him round the neck, his feet off the floor. He threw the desk to the side with such force that it slammed into the wall and stuck in the brickwork like a badly hung piece of modern art. Craig only narrowly avoided joining it, chucking himself on to his stomach across the floor just in time and sliding into a coffee table.

Red's voice played across the walls of the room, threatening to pull it to pieces, brick by brick by brick.

'You should not be here. You should not have come! And to bring Craig? You fool! I sensed something, expected your father, but not you, Lazarus! You must both leave! The Dead are moving, swarming. Something terrible is soon to happen. I have to stop them! Why is the hole in the veil not yet closed?'

Lazarus couldn't speak. All he could do was feel

Red's hand squeezing him, holding him up with impossible ease, his feet swinging uselessly above the floor. The temperature in the room had increased, and Lazarus was sure the ripped ends of peeling wallpaper were starting to smoulder.

'This is a mistake, Lazarus!'

Lazarus was reliving their first meeting, the vomit like reek of Red's breath slipping into his own mouth, causing him to gag. This time Red was more panic and fury than simple, controlled terror.

'You're too valuable! If the Dead find you here . . . What were you thinking? And where is your father? I can sense him, but . . .'

Rage played in Red's eyes, and despite choking, Lazarus could see that with Red's anger so the wounds across his body seemed to break out again, spreading like cracks over a lava field to show the red hot lava beneath.

'I . . . I . . .' managed Lazarus, but nothing more came out. If this went on much longer he'd be unconscious. The bastard was squeezing the life out of him. He tried to fight it, to pull at Red's hand, but it was useless. Red wasn't just strong; it was like trying to wrench a train off its rails with his bare hands.

At last Red released his grip. Lazarus dropped to the floor, coughing hard as he drew breath. His neck was burned and grazed.

'I had no choice!' Lazarus's forehead rested on the floor as he recovered. 'Things have changed.'

'*Nothing* has changed,' hissed Red, ducking his head down to Lazarus's own, pushing it up close like a dog sniffing something dead. 'You got the message to your father, yes? Then where is he? Where is Tobias? Why are the Dead on the move? They are thick outside these walls, Lazarus. They crawl like ants. We are running out of time!'

Lazarus looked up from the floor to face Red. He wasn't going to show any fear, not this time. He'd gone through too much in the past few days to back down to anyone or anything. And whatever Red actually was, he wasn't about to be intimidated.

Lazarus, pushed himself up on to his knees, then hauled himself up to stand and stare Red down.

'I've come for my dad. You were right to sense him, because he's here. Someone or something tricked him into thinking he could open the veil and get Mum back.'

Red turned away from Lazarus, took a few slow steps towards the study door. Lazarus continued speaking. 'He was the start of all this, Red, the one who opened the hole that the Dead are going to flood back through. I need him to help me shut it down. Close the gap he's opened. That's why I'm here. So instead of going crazy, help me!' There he'd said it. All that saving the world crap just faded and disappeared behind this one thing: family. OK, so Dad had never really been any good at the whole parental thing, but he was all Lazarus had. It wasn't much, but he wasn't about to let anyone take it from him. And that was enough to have brought him here to find him.

Red turned back round and stepped forward to face up to Lazarus, his eyes wide and bloodshot into lines like crazy paving. 'You gave him the message? You warned him?'

Lazarus snapped. He was getting tired of not being listened to. 'Are you deaf? Dad's *here*! You were already too late when you came to give him the message and found only me! It was him who punched a hole through the veil!

You haven't got a clue!'

Red slipped across the floor, closer and closer, but Lazarus didn't budge. He wiped spit from his face and didn't blink. Last time all he'd wanted to do was run from Red, but now he wasn't about to back down.

'Impossible,' said Red, turning away from Lazarus and leaving bloody footprints across the floor. 'Tobias is the Keeper! He knows the dangers. He would never risk so much! If he's here, it's to shut it down permanently and sacrifice himself in the process. Foolhardy, but probably effective. But he needs to do it now!'

'Well your precious Keeper – my *dad* – failed!' yelled Lazarus, itching for a fight now even though he knew he'd lose. 'And just so you know, he's not the only Keeper any more. Like I said, you haven't got a clue.'

Red roared. The room fell even darker and the only light Lazarus was suddenly aware of was the horrible fire in Red's eyes like two small furnaces burning with the heat of the sun.

'You are too young! You have not been trained, made ready, shown how to send the Dead back! Don't be a fool!'

'You think I don't know that?' Lazarus spat back, letting his frustration with everything that had happened boil over. It was all he could do not to rip the spike round into the argument and draw blood. 'But it's not like I had any choice – being killed kind of took away my part in the decision-making!'

'Killed? How? Why?'

Lazarus could hear the confusion in Red now. He had the upper hand. He liked the sensation, the power .

At last Craig joined in. 'You'd be better to ask him how many times,' he said. 'And how do you know my name?'

Red didn't even acknowledge Craig, or what he'd said.

'Arielle,' he said. 'Skinny, half-crazy winged alcoholic who carries a big sword? I'm sure you know all about her. She certainly knows all about you.'

Red nodded. Slowly. Deliberately.

'She was looking for Dad too, but couldn't find him. Said she had no choice and shot me. You know, to turn me into the next Keeper by allowing me to taste death just enough to sense it, to *smell* it. That's how this works, isn't it?'

Red nodded again, the intensity in his eyes never

fading. Perhaps burning brighter.

'Next thing I know,' said Lazarus, 'I'm dead and she's bringing me back and I'm the Keeper and I'm fighting off all kinds of crazies trying to kill me again.'

'She should not have killed you,' said Red, voice like a storm just cresting the horizon. 'That was a mistake.'

'The pistol didn't appear in her hand by accident,' said Lazarus. 'Trust me on that.'

'That is not what I meant,' said Red, then he turned again from Lazarus, and walked slowly away.

For a few moments, no one spoke. Craig went to say something, but thought better of it and stayed quiet. Or at least that's what Lazarus guessed happened, as Craig turned to him and did a brilliant goldfish impression.

Lazarus was struck by how Red looked almost sad. Or was he mistaking sadness for fear? It was just about impossible to identify any emotion in such a face. Despite the healing, it was a ruined thing, a mask of horrors remembered for all time.

Red said, 'The car accident that killed your mother … it killed you too.'

Lazarus didn't respond. He wasn't about to let on that

he knew more than Red had guessed. And not just about the accident.

'When you crossed over,' said Red, 'I intervened. Pushed you back.'

Lazarus wasn't sure, but the scar on his arm he'd had since the car accident suddenly seemed to ache. He remembered how Red had reacted when he'd seen it at their first meeting; like he'd recognised it, put it there in the first place.

'Why did you save me?' he asked.

'It was important,' Red replied.

'Important?' said Lazarus, almost mocking. 'That's reassuring.'

'You are the son of the Keeper, Lazarus,' said Red. 'The next in line. Never before had one crossed over before their time, before they had become a Keeper themselves and passed on their knowledge to the next, their own flesh and blood.'

'That's lucky, don't you think?'

'Luck has nothing to do with it,' said Red, and again Lazarus heard an awful rumbling of anger. 'The bloodline of the Keepers is protected utterly by ways and means you cannot possibly comprehend. And I'm not simply talking about the likes of Arielle. To have you die . . .'

Red's voice faded, and Lazarus knew he was hiding something.

'What?' he demanded, his hand reaching down to the spike in his belt. 'What aren't you telling me?'

'Lazarus,' said Red.

'Tell me!' shouted Lazarus, and wrenched the spike from his belt. The metal thorns on the handle slipped through the holes in his hand and out the other side with such ease that it felt to Lazarus more like putting on a glove. But this was a little bit more than that, it could rip skin to shreds in a moment.

Red saw the spike. 'Where did you get that?'

'One of the Dead burrowed into a friend of mine and tried to skewer me with it,' said Lazarus. 'Figured I'd keep it as a souvenir.'

'And you have no idea as to its origins, do you?' said Red.

'All I know is that it's pretty effective at sending the Dead back to where they come from,' Lazarus said with a shrug. 'And that's good enough for me.'

'Your hand,' said Red. He pointed at where the metal thorns from the handle were sticking through Lazarus's skin. 'It does not hurt?'

Lazarus shook his head. 'Now stop changing the subject and tell me what's going on.'

'No Keeper has ever experienced death twice,' said Red. Lazarus noticed how his eyes now and again strayed to the spike. 'No one has. Experiencing it once gives a Keeper the ability to sense the Dead. That's the point.'

'You're not telling me anything I don't already know.'

'But if you experience it twice,' said Red, 'then death already knows who you are.' He paused, like he was trying to give the words time to settle.

'You're making it sound like death is a *thing*,' said Lazarus. 'Next you'll be telling me to keep an eye out for a tall bloke in a black cape carrying a scythe.'

Lazarus found it hard to return Red's stare as he replied. 'Death *is* a thing, Lazarus,' he said. 'Or perhaps it's more accurate to say that it *could* be, if the need arose. It wouldn't be just something you could sense. It would be a part of you.'

Lazarus gripped the spike hard and pointed it at Red's

neck. 'You're beginning to make it sound like I'm one of the four riders of the Apocalypse! Talk sense, Red!'

Red roared. And accompanying that sound, Lazarus saw ripped, burned and broken wings tear from Red's back and crash through the walls of the room before retracting just enough to lift him from the ground.

'Death is in you, Lazarus!' said Red, his voice the echo of walls collapsing. 'Because of what Arielle has done, it is a part of who you are now, as much as your blood, your skin, your very soul!'

'I don't understand,' said Lazarus, backing off a little, and trying his best not to, to not show fear. 'What do you mean?'

Red's wings beat slowly, deliberately, yet caused almost no draft at all. When he spoke again, his voice was low.

'You have become a paradox, Lazarus.'

Lazarus thought he almost saw a faint smile crack that ruined, broken face.

'You are humanity's only protection against an eternal and hopeless death. Yet death is now a part of everything that you are. You could be dangerous, Lazarus. A tangled web is being woven.'

'Are you just trying to scare me?'

'No,' said Red. 'In this, it is you who is scaring me. And that, as I'm sure you can well imagine, is a rare thing indeed.'

Lazarus was stunned. He'd come to find his dad, but now he was being told that he could ruin everything. Quite literally.

A screaming howl, followed by a bellowing roar, crashed through the air. Red turned sharply. It came again, causing both Lazarus and Craig to press their hands in their ears.

'You must leave,' said Red, his wings beating harder now. 'If you are a Keeper, then go back and close the hole in the veil. I will hold the Dead off until you do, though there are more this time than ever before. You are no use to me here!'

'But we can't go back,' said Craig. 'The route's blocked. We've no way out!'

Craig was generally calm about most things, but Lazarus could hear an edge to his voice that was as jagged as a saw blade.

'Then make one!' yelled Red. 'You are the Keeper,

Lazarus! Start being one!'

And before Lazarus or Craig could answer, Red opened his wings and blasted through the wall into whatever lay in the darkness outside.

It took just a little longer than Lazarus expected for the dust to clear.

8

TENTACLES AND TEETH

'I could have lived my whole life happy to have never seen that,' said Craig, as Lazarus dashed to the gaping hole Red had blasted in the wall. The edges of ruined brick looked like broken teeth in a huge and horrible mouth. 'What was all that stuff about you being death? And how *did* he know my name?'

'Red knows everyone's name,' Lazarus replied. 'I'm thinking nothing will ever make sense again. And get a load of this.'

Craig jogged over and stared out through the hole in the wall. 'That's impossible,' he said. 'I mean, that can't actually be real!'

'Well this house is,' said Lazarus, 'so I'm guessing out there is no different.'

'But that's the street outside your house,' said Craig.

'I'd recognise it anywhere, even if it does look like it's only just survived the apocalypse.'

Lazarus couldn't tear his eyes away from the scene now in front of him. It had been one thing to find this house like some solidified part of a dark dream, but to stand here and get an eyeful of the street as well ... Where did it end? Or didn't it? Was this place simply a bad man's dream of what the world was like back in the land of the living? If Lazarus wanted to, would he be able to walk down that road and find himself in other villages and towns and cities he knew, all of them trapped in eternal decay, populated by ... by what? That was a question he was pretty sure he didn't want answering, not least because he had a pretty good idea. He'd seen the Dead, and that thing he'd seen with Craig wasn't the half of it. He knew there were things here that were much, much worse.

'You see Red anywhere?' asked Craig, bringing Lazarus out of his thoughts and back to the now. And the now was the last place either of them wanted to be.

Lazarus shook his head. 'Whatever that howl was, it had him spooked, which isn't a good sign. It sounded close. And he kept on about how the Dead were swarming or something. I can't believe I'm going to say this, but Red . . . he looked almost afraid.'

It made him uneasy thinking it, but it was the truth.

'Yeah, of you,' said Craig. 'So what was it?'

'You don't actually expect me to know the answer, right?'

'No,' said Craig, 'I don't really expect anyone to.'

Lazarus leaned forward to try and get a better look at the street. The houses and buildings and shops, even the church tower in the distance, were all very familiar, but frozen in their last moments before collapse. The roads and pavements were all split with deep rifts. The skeletons of cars and other vehicles lay where they'd died, making the place look like an elephants' graveyard. Where Lazarus remembered grass and trees, all that lay here was mud and ash. The air was damp and stale, like a forest fire was smouldering somewhere far off, and the only light came from the clay-coloured sky as it flashed almost incessantly with white lightning and red flame.

'And why's it so silent out there?' asked Craig.

'Maybe it's the holiday season,' said Lazarus.

'Hmmm,' said Craig, and then he spotted something. 'What's that?' he asked nodding to the far end of the street. 'I can't quite see it because it's so dark. Something's moving, I think.'

'Where?'

Craig pointed and Lazarus followed the line from his Craig's finger into the gloom, like he was pushing it into a dirty puddle. For a few moments, he couldn't see anything, just a thick swirling fog that would occasionally block their view of the street before slouching off to swallow something else with a silent gulp. Then he caught something. A movement, just where Craig had said. But what was it?

'You see it?' asked Craig.

Lazarus nodded. 'Don't know what it is though.'

'Looks like it's coming closer,' said Craig. 'And I'd happily guess that if that's the case, we should get the hell away from here as quickly as possible.'

Lazarus didn't move straight away. He was still staring, trying to see what it was. Sounds were coming from whatever it was. The thing was gaining in speed as it approached. It was gaining in size too.

'That sounds like voices,' said Craig, looking down the street, and Lazarus could hear the fear in Craig's voice. 'Chanting or moaning or something.'

'That's because it is,' said Lazarus at last able to see what it was coming towards them. 'It's the Dead,' he said abruptly. 'And they're coming straight towards us.'

'We're trapped!' said Craig and Lazarus heard desperation and fear in his voice. 'We can't leave the house because they'll see us. And we can't go back the way we came, because there *is* no back-the-way-we-came! Not unless you know how to break through, like Red pretty much said you could.'

'You'd think he could've told me how, wouldn't you?' said Lazarus.

'Leaves us with little choice then, really,' said Craig.

Lazarus nodded, now thinking only of getting out, getting away, staying alive. 'Back to the rubble. We might be able to find a way through. It's a long shot, but it's our only one.'

The chanting was growing in volume now and sounded anything but friendly.

'Come on!' said Lazarus, and grabbed Craig by the

shoulder and made to move out of the study when he remembered: 'But the steps! They collapsed!'

Another loud moan from outside drowned out Craig's despairing disappointment, but then, through the moan, a horrifying and utterly human scream cut through.

'I really don't want to know who or what made that sound,' said Craig as they both turned back to the hole in the wall.

Lazarus dashed back to stare out. The crowd was closer now. They seemed to be fighting each other to get to the front, kicking and screaming and punching and pulling at each other. A rabble of madness. Were they trying to get somewhere? Or away from something?

'Something else is coming,' said Lazarus. 'That scream wasn't from the crowd. It was from over there.' He pointed down the street, or what was left of it.

Lazarus stared down the street and saw nothing. Just more swirling darkness.

A ripping clatter snapped Lazarus back to the crowd and he recoiled instinctively. The fight had just upped a gear. One of the Dead was now being passed across the raised hands of the crowd. They were pulling and clawing at it, and bits were coming away. Not just clothing, but chunks of flesh, then a hand, an arm . . .

Another howl.

And what Lazarus saw hurtling towards them brought back the nightmare that had started this only a few days ago, yet it felt like years.

Red was riding a wave of his Creatures of Oblivion – his hounds as he'd called them – like he was surfing a tsunami of tentacles and teeth. The sound was deafening, with the leathery beat of Red's ruined wings, and the wet, flapping tumble of the giant octopus-like creatures sweeping through the air. Then they were on the Dead and the world turned a thick, bloody red.

Lazarus tried to turn Craig away from what was happening. 'Don't look. You don't want to watch. Seriously, mate, just turn away. Now.'

Craig seemed unable to obey. He stood there, mouth gaping, as Red and his creatures disappeared from sight as the crowd of the Dead swamped him.

Lazarus remembered then how he'd felt when he'd first seen these creatures Red had referred to as his pets.

He hadn't been sure which had been more terrifying: the Dead themselves, or Red's Creatures of Oblivion. It had all been so overwhelmingly impossible, the shock of it jarring hideously against normal life he had, up until that point, been living. Everything had changed then, hadn't it? Red's arrival, the Dead, the creatures. From that moment on, even on the brightest of days, Lazarus knew he would always be aware of the darkness.

Lazarus yanked Craig away from the terrible scene, and Craig eventually gave way, collapsing in on himself. They both dropped to the floor.

'Laz ... what the hell were those things?' Craig's voice was shaking and he was only just managing to stop going into full meltdown. 'All those tentacles and teeth or thorns or ... What in hell's name were they? We need to get out, Laz! We need to get out of here now!'

The sounds from outside grew more sickening, forcing Lazarus and Craig to block their ears. Just when Lazarus felt he could take no more, when he found himself wondering if his dad was lost for good, if he'd ever find him – the din was sucked to silence like water down a plug hole.

Lazarus felt his ears pop, squeezed his eyes tight shut, saw stars. When he opened them again, Craig was shaking his head and trying to stand up. Lazarus pushed himself to his feet. The sudden silence was almost tangible, like he could reach out and touch it or prod it.

With a few hesitant steps, Lazarus stumbled up to the hole in the wall and peered out, not yet willing to step further. The air swilling in from outside was thick, like heat reflected off a beach, and with every breath he tasted stale dust. He coughed, wiped his eyes, aware of a silence that crawled across his skin like spiders. The street was hushed, and he could see the Dead standing like those awaiting the passing of a funeral hearse. Or a queen. In their very centre, Lazarus saw Red. He was back to how Lazarus remembered him – a bloody figure, short of breath, wings back; and he was standing on his hounds as though they were all that were stopping him from collapsing. Lazarus was aware of a sound hushing and shuffling its way forward from his right. He couldn't see what it was because of where he was stood. The only way to check it out properly was to get outside.

Steeling himself for whatever lay outside, Lazarus

buried his fear and before he oculd change his mind, dashed from the room, bowled out of what was left of the front door, and ran down the broken path. At the bottom, he stopped to see what had brought the fight between Red and the Dead to a stop.

Another crowd. They were further away and difficult to see clearly, though they moved slowly and with a quieter purpose. At the front, Lazarus could make out a hooded figure all in white. Directly behind the white figure, a group of other similarly dressed creatures – though in grey, not white – carried above them a large square frame constructed from wood and scrap metal and tied together with twisted, black twine.

Lazarus strained his eyes to see what was hanging on the frame. One thing he knew: it was important to the Dead. He squinted, looked harder. And then, despite it being too far away to make out in detail, the thing took shape.

It was a body.

9

DEATH DIVE

Lazarus snapped round to bolt inside, but Craig was jogging down the path towards him. And what he saw coming up behind Craig made him stop like he'd run into a brick wall: a thick crowd of the Dead was silently slipping down the side of the house, oozing towards them both.

Lazarus went to scream a warning at Craig, but he stopped himself. The Dead didn't seem to be interested in either of them, and were heading to the road. Their disguise of corpse clothes was about to get seriously tested.

'Laz, what's going on, mate? What's happening?'

Lazarus didn't need to answer. The Dead were finally upon them. They could do nothing.

'Shit!'

They both felt the Dead brush past them, clambering over each other to get to whatever was happening in the street.

'Don't react!' Lazarus whispered urgently. 'I'm hoping these disguises keep us hidden long enough to think up a way out of this.'

A thick swarm of the Dead were around them now. Unless they wanted to fight against the flow, they had no choice but to allow themselves to be taken along, through what was left of the garden wall and out in the street.

Craig was shivering with fear. 'Our disguises didn't work with that thing in the cavern, did they? And now we're right in the middle of some kind of Dead protest march!'

'But that thing in the cavern wasn't like these,' said Lazarus.

'What, you mean, dead?' said Craig.

'I think there are different types of the Dead,' said Lazarus. 'Some seem to be like these here; just stumbling around like God knows what. Others . . .'

'Others *what*?' asked Craig, clearly trying to calm down.

'Look,' said Lazarus, 'I just don't think it's as simple as there being one kind. Some Dead are different, more powerful, more . . . bad, I guess. You saw that blacksmith, right? The one that attacked us when we were with Arielle?'

The look on Craig's face told Lazarus he'd never forget it. That thing had been a giant, an impossible creature in a stained leather apron that Lazarus had only just stopped. It was the kind of thing that scarred a memory like a chainsaw.

The Dead continued to flood past, more and more coming from everywhere now, pushing past them, knocking into them. Their true horror was now up close and personal, revealing what was left when humanity had gone. Their clothes, like everything else here, were fixed in decay. Their skin didn't fit right. Some seemed more damaged than others, like they wore the scars of what had killed them. Lazarus gagged when he felt something brush past his feet: a charred body pulling itself forward, the last remaining threads of a seatbelt strapped round it and attached to the skeleton of a car seat.

Craig leaned in. 'What are they doing?'

Lazarus nodded towards the body strapped to the frame. 'Don't make it obvious that you're staring,' he said, 'but that's got something to do with it. From what I can make out, it seems they've grabbed one of their own and strapped it to that thing. I don't know why, and I'm pretty sure I don't want to find out.'

'What about Red?'

Lazarus was already tiring of trying to make sense of the impossible. 'He's here to stop the Dead. I don't know what the Dead are intending to do. And as for those creatures under him, you're probably best off not knowing any more than you already do, OK?'

'Agreed,' said Craig.

'Good,' Lazarus replied. 'To be honest, I'm just amazed we're still alive. Seems my dad's idea of wearing this stuff actually worked.'

'What about your dad?' asked Craig. 'I mean, you came here to find him, right?'

'And you,' said Lazarus.

'I know,' said Craig, 'but you were coming anyway. I just got in the way. What now?'

'For now we make like the Dead,' said Lazarus, 'and

wait this out. It's our only chance.'

'Shut up!' said Craig, his voice rising in volume. 'Are you mental? We need to find another way back! We wait round here, something bad is going to happen. And by bad, I'm thinking serious gut-munching and skull-crunching!'

'These aren't zombies in the movies,' snapped Lazarus.

'No, they're worse!' Craig's face was lined with fear. 'These are *real*!'

'And if we turn and go the opposite way,' said Lazarus, keeping his voice low, 'if we go against the crowd, they'll notice us. We can't risk it.'

'But they'll kill us!' said Craig. 'Seriously, Laz, this is nuts! We need to bolt. Like now!'

Craig turned, but Lazarus pulled him back.

'We need Red!' he said, drilling his eyes into his friend. 'Other than my dad, he's the only one this side of the veil who can help us get back. When this is over, we need to find him or . . .'

Lazarus didn't want to think about what would happen to them if they couldn't get back through the veil.

'Shut up!'

'I'm telling the truth!' Lazarus knew he was shouting now. 'We can't go back through the house. Our route is blocked. Neither of us knows where to go next, how to get back. So either we go hide in the house and hope this all goes away – and I'm thinking it probably won't – or we stick around and wait till we can get to Red!'

'But—'

'There's no argument on this,' Lazarus snapped back. 'I'm the Keeper. It's my decision!'

For the next few seconds, neither spoke. Laz knew his words had stung Craig and he immediately regretted how they'd come out. He hadn't meant to sound so pissed off. And he couldn't expect Craig to understand what was going on; he wasn't even supposed to be here! In their many years of friendship they'd hardly ever fallen out, and they'd certainly never argued like this. But this was different. He had to take charge. He just needed Craig to trust him.

Another scream of agony came from the figure strapped to the frame. Lazarus had never really thought about the Dead feeling pain. But then he'd never really expected to see one of them treated in such a way. It was like watching a scene from medieval history.

'Is it a man or a woman?' asked Craig.

'I can't make it out. And to be honest, I'm not sure I want to hang around to find out.'

'Maybe this is the kind of thing that happens here all the time?' said Lazarus.

'Which is a bloody good reason for us to get the hell out of here asap,' said Craig.

Lazarus wasn't about to disagree. But he was still sticking to his decision that Red was their best chance. He just had to get to him once this was over. Though how he was going to do that in this crowd he still hadn't decided.

Then, as if answering his thoughts, Lazarus saw Red stretch out his wings. With a flap that sent out a tornado to scatter the Dead around him, he shot straight up into the air. For a moment he paused, hovering above the street, casting it in shadow. Then with a wild howl he pulled his wings back against his body, like a hawk in a death dive aiming for the kill, and swooped through the crowd towards the person on the frame, wings slicing through the Dead like a scythe through corn.

10

BROKEN BODIES

'Down!' yelled Lazarus.

He wasn't sure if Red was going to stop, but the wave of blood-drenched destruction he was bringing with him was something Lazarus didn't want to be swamped by. If those wings caught them, they'd be sliced in half. Red didn't know they were there, thought they'd headed back through the veil after their little chat; and even if he did, Lazarus had no idea if he'd stop.

The Dead were shrieking and crying as Red drove through them. The crowd was so thick that none could escape. Lazarus grabbed Craig and dropped them both to the floor as the Dead around them did nothing to get away from what was happening. He felt a blast of wind shoot over them, slicing the air where they had been standing only a second earlier. The Dead fell about them and on top of them: a screaming pile of broken bodies blown apart by Red.

'Laz,' whispered Craig, 'you're crushing me!'

Lazarus rolled left, allowed Craig to breathe. In the process he dislodged the bits of the Dead that had landed on him. Was he already getting desensitised to it, he thought, as he flicked a messed-up hand off his leg and turned away from a severed head, not least because the eyes in the thing were still moving?

'You OK?'

Craig nodded as best he could. 'Give me a bit more warning next time you're going to do that, though, OK? I cracked my head when we landed.'

'Sorry mate,' said Lazarus. 'It was either that or be sliced in two. Red's really going all out to stop the Dead getting any further in what they're doing.'

'I'll take the headache,' said Craig. 'Hey – it's gone quiet again.'

Lazarus slowly raised his head to see what was going on. And what he saw made him feel like he'd woken up on a battlefield. Bodies were strewn everywhere. The Dead who'd survived stood amongst the carnage like solitary trees, swaying slightly, dazed by what had happened. Although he was still too far away to make out exactly what was going on, Lazarus could see Red standing in front of the white and grey figures holding the body on the frame.

In front of them stood Red.

'What is it?' asked Craig and joined Lazarus to have a look.

'Whatever it is,' said Lazarus, 'I think it's to do with the one they've got on the frame. And it's probably not very nice.'

Lazarus heard a voice, but couldn't make out any words.

'They're speaking,' he said. 'Red and the one all in white.'

'What are they saying?'

'It's too quiet,' said Lazarus trying to hear, but not catching nothing, not a word. 'We're too far away.'

The surviving Dead were all facing Red and the white figure. Lazarus saw one very close to him sniff and then stick out its tongue like it was tasting the air. Then it turned slowly to look down at him and Craig.

'I think we have a problem,' said Lazarus and elbowed Craig hard.

The Dead's eyes were now so wide it looked like its eyelids had been removed.

'If that one's noticed us,' whispered Craig, 'then it's probably not the only one. What the hell are we going to do?'

Lazarus pulled the spike from his belt. The sensation of the thorns on the handle slipping through his hand was little comfort. He could only take on a few of them.

'When it comes for us,' he said trying to sound confident, 'let me deal with it. I'll take it down, then we bolt.'

'Where to?'

'Anywhere that's away from here!' Lazarus hissed. 'Ready?'

Craig nodded, but then, as they both readied themselves for the fight, the Dead turned back to Red.

Lazarus looked back towards Red again wondering what had distracted them. He could see with a glance that all the other Dead were doing the same, staring towards Red, like they were waiting for something. After what had just happened, what else could there be to see? The white figure's voice rose. So did Red's. Lazarus could hear them both clearly now, but couldn't make out any words. Whatever they were saying, it was wrapped up in a language of snarls and guttural cries that snapped and bit at each other like fighting alligators.

'They're arguing about something,' said Lazarus and Craig stretched up to have a look. 'And they're both just standing there, facing each other. It's like they're both waiting for the other to attack first.'

'So who's that one in the white?' asked Craig. 'And what's that body strapped up on that frame got to do with any of this? I thought the land of the Dead was just, you know, dead. I didn't think it would be like this. And I've watched a lot of horror movies.'

Lazarus didn't respond. He felt just the same as Craig about where they were and what they'd seen. If he thought about it too much, he wondered if he'd be able to deal with it at all and not just let panic take over and pull him to pieces.

The figure in white raised a hand and pointed it at the body hanging on the frame. A bellow from Red did nothing. Lazarus and Craig saw a shadow fall on the scene and blank it out completely.

Craig spoke first. 'What the hell's that?'

Lazarus stared at it, but the darkness was giving nothing away. But he had a horrible feeling that whatever was taking place, it was something that he and Craig should be as far away from as possible. It was bad; he could smell it on the air. Not quite the usual stench of death, but more cloying and suffocating.

Craig said, 'Mate, whatever's going on, it looks like even Red's lost. We have to get out of here.'

'But I don't know how!' said Lazarus, 'I haven't a clue!'

'You'll think better if we're not here,' said Craig, and grabbed Lazarus's arm. 'Come on – back to the house!'

A scream ripped from the black hole of darkness, but still nothing. What was happening? What was Red doing?

'Seriously, Laz!' shouted Craig, pulling at Lazarus. 'We need to move – now!'

But something was holding Lazarus's attention. Something about the darkness that he couldn't draw his eyes away from. There was something in it that he had to see, even if it burned out his eyes to do so.

'Laz!'

Lazarus snatched his arm away, started to wade towards the black. If he could get a little closer, maybe then he could make it out.

Craig yelled at him to stop, but Lazarus ignored him. Even when he heard his friend following, tripping and slipping on the bodies under foot, he still pushed forward.

Soon, Lazarus could make out Red, just standing, frozen almost. And the figure in white.

But it was the body on the frame that he was drawn to. There was something about it that made him cold to the core.

11

☠ DEAD POOL EYES ☠

'**D**AD!'
Lazarus's voice burst out of him with such ferocity that it scraped his throat sore in a second. He yelled again, but his voice simply broke, fell to nothing but a weak cry. That body . . . it was his father!

He and Craig weren't the only ones who heard it. As one, the Dead turned from Lazarus's dad on the frame to glare at them, their eyes like black suns burning.

And so did Red.

Lazarus was trapped by Red's stare. His eyes were pulled wide with shock and anger. Lazarus had no idea what to do now. The look on Red's face felt like it would burn him to nothing on the spot.

A cry from Red split the night and his wings snapped out. The Creatures of Oblivion burst into life. Almost as if they were expecting it, the Dead surged once more. Red's initial attack had not done enough. There were too many of them. Lazarus knew that now. And he watched, stunned and horrified, as Red and his hounds were swamped – then slowly, impossibly, dragged away.

'Laz . . .'

Craig's voice sounded distant. All Lazarus could do was watch Red disappear, dragged off by the crowds. Without him, what hope did they have at all of getting out of here?

'Laz,' said Craig again, and Lazarus felt his friend pulling at his sleeve. 'You need to work out a way of getting us back to the land of the Living. Red's no use to us now. Come on . . .'

Lazarus could think of nothing to say. His dad was as good as dead. And now their only other chance of staying alive was being dragged away to who knew where.

'I know this is going to be the last thing you want to do,' said Craig, trying again to get Lazarus's attention, 'but we're really in the shit now and need an exit quick!'

'I need to get Dad,' said Lazarus. 'I need to get him down!'

He tried to pull away from Craig's grasp, but Craig held him tight. He could feel his world was ending, falling in flames to soot and darkness. The only thing that had kept him going, helped him make any sense of this, was the thought that he was doing it only to find his dad and start over. But now . . . what was left? All that saving-the-world crap Arielle had spoken of meant nothing. Nothing at all. In that moment, as far as Lazarus was concerned, the world could burn.

'I can't let you do that, Laz,' Craig said. 'You're our only chance now of getting home!'

'I came here for him!' yelled Laz. Hot tears were now scorching down his cheeks. Why wasn't Craig going to help him? 'I can't just leave him, can I? They're killing him, Craig! He's my bloody dad!'

'You think I don't know that?' Craig shouted back. 'But do you really think he wants to see you dead too? Think, Laz! We can't do anything! Not here! Not now!'

Again Craig pulled at Lazarus, and again Lazarus stayed his ground.

'You can't make me!' It was all Lazarus could do not to punch Craig to the ground and go it alone. 'He's my dad. He's why I'm here!'

Without warning, Craig slapped Lazarus across the cheek with the back of his hand. It came out of nowhere, split Lazarus's lip and stung like hell. Shocked, Lazarus stumbled, tripped and fell.

'See some bloody sense!' yelled Craig, his words spitting from him like sparks from a fire. 'If you go after your dad, we're all dead, you hear me? Dead! You really want that? Would *he*?'

Lazarus responded by pulling out the spike and, with a cry, launching himself at Craig.

Craig didn't have time to duck or move, just stood there as Lazarus pushed him violently to the ground, and with a roar, drove the spike into the chest of one of the Dead as it closed in on them. Lazarus guessed it had once been a man. Now it was a thing with the back of its head missing. He'd seen it almost too late, but just soon enough to stop him before he got his hands on Craig.

The Dead shuddered, trying to pull itself off the spike, but it wasn't going anywhere. Lazarus rammed the weapon deeper, felt it slip in easily until it was in all the way up to the handle. The creature's breath was foul and he tried to claw at Lazarus. With a wrench, Lazarus twisted the spike. He felt flesh and bone give way. The Dead squealed like an animal caught in a snare. Lazarus twisted again and wrenched the spike hard to the right. The force of the move threw the Dead away from Lazarus to land on its back. It tried to get up again, but the wound left by the spike was growing, creeping across its body. The Dead looked confused and shook violently, until at last it stopped and lay very, very still. Finally the body gave up and fell apart like all the major joints had come unglued.

Lazarus, bloody spike in his hand, turned to Craig. 'You OK?'

Craig nodded, wasn't given time to say anything, as another of the Dead attacked. This one had once been a woman, and was dressed in the last threads of an expensive dress, hair half falling out of its head. Craig swung his legs round hard and tripped it up as it lunged for Lazarus. Instinctively, Lazarus rammed the spike in with such force that it drove right through the Dead, his hand and arm following right up to his shoulder. The Dead's face registered mild surprise as Lazarus looked up into its dead pool eyes.

'They're all coming,' said Craig. 'The house isn't far away, but our chances of getting there . . .'

The Dead clawed at Lazarus as he tried to pull himself free.

'Craig!'

Craig grabbed the thing's arm and with a heave, ripped it from Lazarus. The force sent the creature spinning across the ground to land on its front. And by the time it landed it was dissolving.

'I didn't think it was possible to kill something that was already dead,' said Craig, edging up to Lazarus's side as more of the Dead approached. They looked hungry.

'It's not,' replied Lazarus. He focused on the feel of the spike in his hand, how the thorns jabbing through the back of his hand seemed to become more deadly with every moment. 'You can destroy the body they've created to live in, but that doesn't get rid of them completely. They come back eventually, when they've regained enough strength.'

'So we're fighting a losing battle?'

Lazarus shrugged. 'I don't know what we're fighting,' he said. 'I just want my dad back.'

'Then do something to get us out of here!'

Lazarus's reply was cut off as arms bound round his neck like a snake. Craig leapt to help, but was held back by something grabbing his foot.

Lazarus struggled against whatever it was that was holding him, but it wasn't letting go. The strange arms were squeezing hard, and it felt like they were starting to seep into him and become a part of what he was. The thought that one of the Dead could take over his body like a new tenant was too much. With every ounce of strength he had, he slammed his head backwards. Whatever it connected with, gave way and squashed like a nut between a hammer and a stone. Lazarus twisted right, pulled himself free, and used his momentum to bring the spike round to finish off what he'd started. This time it wasn't the main blade that did the job, but the thorns jutting out from the back of his hand. And they tore into the mashed head of the Dead which had attacked him.

It took Lazarus a couple of seconds to pull his hand free. When he finally managed to, he caught sight of something far off. There was a ripple of movement in the crowd that had taken Red. Like a missile shot from a submarine, Red burst upwards from the sea of the Dead, sending them scattering.

'Either that's the cavalry,' said Craig, 'or we're about to be finished off real quick.'

'I think it's the cavalry,' said Lazarus as Red turned in the sky and raced down on a collision course for the figure in white.

Lazarus's dad still hung high on the wooden frame. His body was limp now, hardly breathing. The jet of darkness had stopped. But as Red closed in, the figure in white turned back to his dad and, with a scream that sounded like a lioness being ripped apart, pointed both hands at him. A thick black column of darkness burst from the figure's palms.

Lazarus screamed as the darkness slammed into his dad. It spilled all over him, cutting into and out of him, like it was trying to thread him with black ribbons.

Lazarus went to run forward, to do something – *anything* – but hands grabbed his legs. He kicked, lashed out with the spike, but he couldn't move.

As he struggled to break free, he watched helplessly as his father pulled in desperation against the wires cutting into his wrists and ankles.

Red was only seconds away when Lazarus, for a split second, caught his father's eyes. It wasn't much, but in that moment, so much travelled between them that he almost fell backwards with the shock of it.

He saw the father he'd never known; a man who'd held a terrible secret and mourned the death of his wife in silence and solitude all his life. A father who loved him but had never known how, nor been able, to show it. A father, who in that moment, opened his mouth and whimpered a single word.

'Lazarus . . .'

Then Lazarus saw his father's shoulders drop, his body sag, and the dark swamp him completely. A moment later, the frame was empty.

His dad's body was gone.

12

RIPPED APART

'No!' Lazarus's yell burst from him, his legs gave way, and he collapsed to his knees. He blinked, rubbed his eyes, stared at the frame. But it was empty, and no amount of staring would turn that fact to fiction. His dad was gone, destroyed by that spew of darkness.

'Dad . . .'

Lazarus could say no more. Every thought he had about his father, every emotion and feeling, was scorched to a cinder and blown to the wind. He'd just seen his life ripped apart. Grief chased through his mind for a moment, but was soon mixing with a black empty rage.

And standing beneath the frame, he could see the person responsible: the one in white.

Craig knelt down next to Laz, put an arm

round him to help him up.

'Come on, mate,' he said, voice quiet, 'we've got to get out of this.'

Lazarus was sobbing, anger twisting him, grief clawing at his skin. It felt like every part of his body was pushing out tears. He was shaking: it was impossible to stop.

'Laz,' said Craig again, this time standing up, heaving Lazarus to his feet, 'we need to move. They're on to us again.'

Lazarus struggled against Craig and shook him free. 'That bastard killed my dad!' he spat, jabbing the spike in the direction of the one all in white. The Dead were turning slowly now to face him and Craig.

Craig tried to hold Lazarus, but it was no good. Lazarus was out of his hands in a second, twisting away from him, almost stumbling and falling in the process.

'Don't be an idiot, Laz!' Craig yelled, looking round at the Dead, then wading after Lazarus. 'You saw what happened to your dad! We need to get back, speak to Arielle!'

'Not before I've threaded that bastard on to this.' Laz clenched the spike harder, poured his hate and his anger and his utter sense of loss into it, every dark emotion and drive he could find within himself. He felt the thorns on the handle jab him, grow again, like they were feeding off him. And then, almost inexplicably, he became aware of two things. The warmth of his own blood flowing again down his arm, and . . .

The *veil*.

Lazarus pushed tears from his eyes with bloodied hands and tried to clear his mind. He knew they'd come through the veil in the cavern under his house. That's where it was and the way back was blocked. So why could he sense it now? Red had told him he could push back through from wherever he was because he was the Keeper, but how? He thought harder, tried to piece together what he knew, but it did no good. Neither did it alter the fact that now, in this moment, he sensed that he could make the veil appear in front of him and simply step through it. But that was nonsense, wasn't it? The veil was where they'd seen it. Making it appear on a whim didn't make any sense at all!

Lazarus was deep in thought when he heard a yell.

'Laz! Look out!'

One of the Dead leapt up and drove itself at Lazarus. Lazarus didn't even flinch. He extended his arm, caught the thing on the spike, wrenched hard and tossed it away, its torso all but in two pieces. He turned again towards the figure in white, ignoring his thoughts about the veil – but Craig pulled him back. Lazarus snapped round, could feel his whole body burning with what he was going to do to the person who'd killed his dad.

'It's me!' Craig shouted. 'You have to listen to me, Laz! Seriously! We've got to get out!'

Lazarus pulled away, but Craig stopped him, heaved him back. Then something came for Lazarus out of the shadows. Craig saw the Dead thing coming, knocked Lazarus out of the way and grabbed its head. It was wearing the shredded, mouldy remnants of a business suit. A suitcase was attached to its wrist by a chain, and flapped open uselessly. The Dead tore at Craig, its teeth gnashing, but Craig held on. Then, out of nowhere, Lazarus sank the spike into the thing's right eye and out the back of its head.

As Lazarus yanked the spike out, Craig dropped the body. They both watched as it started to crack and fall apart. Within seconds it was rotting away to nothing. The last thing to disappear was the look of shock scribed into its face and mouth.

'They're all after us now,' said Craig, turning to Lazarus. 'Look around you!'

At last, Lazarus listened to his friend. They were surrounded, and the way to the figure in white was blocked by the Dead. But something was different about them. The way they were staring, behaving, seemed almost hesitant. Scared. Why?

Lazarus was suddenly very aware of the spike in his hand. When he'd first seen it, back in the hospital when Clair had attacked him, it had seemed to be nothing more than a weapon made of metal. But here, now, it felt like something more. Powerful. He brought it up to eye level.

'They're not attacking,' said Craig. 'What's going on?'

Lazarus pointed the spike at the Dead closest to them. They shuffled backwards as best they could, like they were wary, and Lazarus knew it was the spike they were afraid of. What did they know about it that he didn't?

'It's this,' he said, looking at Craig. 'It's like they recognise it. They're afraid of it. Or us. Or both.'

'We do look pretty scary,' said Craig. He raised his hands like a tiger. 'Grrrr ...'

Lazarus couldn't help himself; a faint smile slipped across his face. Even in the face of all this, Craig had an uncanny ability to turn a laugh out of it. It didn't kill the grief or quench the anger, but it made him still feel human. And he wasn't even going to let what had happened to his dad stop that. Lazarus figured most people would find that insensitive or inappropriate. But he wasn't most people. And Craig knew him better than anyone else.

That brief moment of respite brought a clarity to Lazarus's mind. He pushed the overwhelming grief he felt for his dad deep down inside. There would be tears another time. But not now. Not if they wanted to get out of this place alive.

'You're right,' he said, turning to face Craig. 'We have to get back to Arielle. Maybe she can explain this, maybe not. But that's our best chance.'

Lazarus saw the look in Craig's eyes – one of a slim chance of hope.

'You mean you think you can get us out of here?'

Lazarus was hesitant, tried again to work out why he

could sense the veil. 'I'm not sure,' he began, his voice quiet, his eyes scanning the Dead still standing away from them. 'It's just that when I was going after that person who killed Dad, I felt something.'

'What?'

Lazarus held up the spike. 'This,' he said. 'I can't explain it, but it's as if this is becoming a part of me. For a moment back then, I was sure I could sense the veil, like I could pretty much drag it here now and push through. I know that sounds crazy . . .'

'To be honest,' said Craig, 'that word has no meaning anymore.'

Lazarus said, 'It was just a feeling. I might have made it up. It might be nothing.'

A thunder clap sent them both into each other as the ground shook. Around them, the Dead fell like dominoes.

'What *now*?' hissed Craig. 'I'm getting tired of all the big noises and dramatic silences!'

Lazarus was up quick. Something was coming. He could feel it.

And then he saw it: far off, something was speeding towards them.

Craig turned. And they both recognised what was shooting towards them at the same time.

'It's Red,' said Lazarus.

'And he's coming right for us,' said Craig.

Neither had a chance to react. No sooner had they seen him than Red was on them. The Dead were scattered like confetti and Lazarus felt himself gripped by rock-hard arms and swept skyward, his stomach left way, way below as his breath was sucked dry.

13

☠☠ BENT AND BROKEN ☠☠

Lazarus lost all awareness of height as Red pulled them up into the billowing clouds above. The higher they got, the worse the air tasted, and Lazarus felt like his mouth was filled with ash. For a moment, he was reminded of being at school as a child, doing an art lesson with charcoal, sucking the stuff like a pencil while he thought about what to draw. It had broken off in his mouth; tasted burned, dry.

Red brought them to a dead stop and Lazarus felt like he was on a rollercoaster, that sensation of being at the top of the highest drop just a split second before the car topples forward, your stomach already ahead of you, drawing you onwards. The childhood memory fizzed to nothing. In the pause before the inevitable fall, Lazarus looked down.

He was staring at a satellite picture of his dead

hometown. Lazarus recognised most of it, despite how damaged the whole place was. From up here it was like staring at cracks in ice, as roads snapped off into the distance at all angles. He could see the ruined marketplace, cars burning in the car park between the library and the river, a train crashed off the rails. And he could make out the Dead too; crowds of them milling through the place, rioting and burning. But if he looked to the edges of the town, the land around was green or pleasant. It was a blackened wasteland home to only storms and winds ripping through.

'I told you to leave,' said Red, turning to look at Lazarus.

'I didn't know how!' Lazarus replied. 'The way back was blocked. And I wanted . . . I *needed*, to find Dad.'

Red said no more. Turning from Lazarus, he arched his back, wings outstretched. Lazarus's stomach dropped again as his world turned upside down. Without warning, Red pulled his wings in. Lazarus felt them wrap around the three of them tightly, blocking out all light. Then acceleration took over and Lazarus closed his eyes.

For a few moments, the only sound was that of wind

squealing past on the other side of Red's wings. Unless Red pulled up, they were going to slam into the ground. What was he doing – trying to kill them?

Lazarus felt a thick thump hurtle through Red's body and his own. They slowed down; then with a final jolt, came to a dead stop. Red's wings unfurled and Lazarus rolled on to a stony floor.

Deep breaths . . .

Lazarus lay for a few seconds. Still. Quiet. The only sound he could hear was breathing – Craig's and Red's, though Red's breath rattled horribly like something beyond repair. Lazarus checked himself to make sure nothing was broken: wriggled a toe, slowly turned his head left-right-left, then brought up the hand that was still holding the spike. He was in one piece, and that was something at least. But when he checked on Craig and Red, he was met with carnage.

Whatever colour Craig's clothes had been before, whatever muck and grime had covered him, it was all gone. Now, in its place, was blood. Red's blood.

'Laz,' whispered Craig, propping himself up on his elbow. 'What the hell happened? Where are we?'

'You OK?' asked Lazarus, ignoring Craig's question. 'I mean, you look ... terrible.' Craig glanced at himself, checked out his hands. 'Where the hell has all this come from? It's not mine – it can't be! I know it isn't!'

Lazarus let his eyes fall to the body lying between them.

'Shit,' muttered Craig. 'Is he ... dead?'

'I don't think there's an accurate answer to that,' replied Lazarus.

Red looked like he'd been thrown down a mountain. His limbs and his wings were bent and broken, twisting out at wrong angles. All over his skinless body were deep gashes like rifts and crevasses in an ice flow. They seeped with an unstoppable flow of blood, and the pool was spreading outwards underneath them all, thick and dark and sticky. And warm.

Lazarus stood up. He took in the car wreck and the shimmering surface of the veil. 'We're back in the cavern,' he said.

'We can't be,' said Craig. 'How?'

Lazarus could feel a breeze brushing him. He looked up to see where it was coming from, and was faced with a hole in the ceiling of the cavern.

'Red punched a way through,' he said, and pointed upwards.

'No way,' Craig said, staring. 'He punched through who knows how many metres of rock? Just like that? He couldn't have! He's not a bunker-buster missile!'

'But he did,' said Lazarus, looking back at Red. 'And it doesn't look like it did him much good.'

For the first time since meeting Red, Lazarus actually felt something other than terror in his presence. It wasn't pity, at least he didn't think it was, but it was as though he was seeing beyond how Red looked and acted. Had he been like Arielle once?

A groaning slipped down through the hole from above.

Craig looked at Laz. 'I don't mean to sound ominous, but I think the Dead are coming.'

Lazarus turned from Craig, looked at the veil. 'I've achieved nothing,' he said. 'Dad's dead. The veil . . . I still don't know how to close it.'

'Then ask Arielle when we get back,' said Craig, as another moan came, this time louder, closer. Lazarus could hear Craig's voice hurrying now; he wanted them back on the other side before anything else crazy happened. 'I don't believe for a minute she doesn't have some idea how to do it. But now Red's brought us here, I reckon we should get a shift on.'

'But Arielle doesn't know,' said Lazarus. 'She told me that before I crossed over. Why would she say otherwise? That's why I needed Dad.'

'It doesn't matter anymore!' said Craig, whipping round on Lazarus now. 'This discussion is over and we'll sort this out on the other side. You came here to rescue me and I'm not about to let you stop us getting back. I've got a life, Laz, and it doesn't end here. Understand?'

'You don't know what you're saying.'

'Yes I do,' said Craig, his voice calmer but no less forceful. 'So shut up and move. Or am I going to have to drag you, kicking and screaming?'

Lazarus hesitated, saw the stony look on Craig's face, and headed towards the veil. But as he did, a movement stopped him. He looked over at Red, saw his eyes fall open and stare. Then he coughed.

'Red could've saved Dad,' said Lazarus, his voice quiet and his eyes focused on Red coming round on the ground.

Cold anger flared in him again, just like in the moments after he'd seen his dad blasted to nothing. 'Why didn't he even try?'

Red coughed again, spitting something black and purple that splattered across the floor. He tried to roll on to his side. But Lazarus didn't give him a chance. He jumped on to him, sat on his chest to pin down his arms. Then he raised the fist holding the spike, and brought it down in a hard punch across Red's face. The thorns jabbing through his hand ripped and tore into Red.

Lazarus pulled his hand back and thrust the spike under Red's chin.

'What the hell are you doing, Laz?' said Craig, shocked. 'He just saved us!'

Lazarus ignored Craig. He was getting good at it. He leaned in close to Red, ignored the fresh wound he'd just brought to that awful face. 'I should kill you now,' he said, pushing the spike just a little harder. 'You could've saved my father.'

Red bubbled up a laugh. It sounded like a drain overflowing. Laz pushed again. Red flinched, but laughed louder.

'Why didn't you save him? Why? Tell me now, before I stick this thing through your stupid, skinned head and turn you into a kebab!'

And at that, Red roared. The laugh bounced and rolled around the cavern until it finally escaped through the hole Red had bored through from above.

'You are so like your father,' said Red, turning to face Lazarus.

Rage lit Lazarus like a flare and he punched Red again. But all it did was make Red laugh harder still, despite the added injury.

'Don't you see, Lazarus?' Red chuckled. 'You both risked coming through the veil for love: he for his wife, you for him, for Craig.'

'It's not funny!' yelled Lazarus and raised his fist again, but this time it was brought to a halt as it came in for another hit: Red had caught it. Lazarus struggled and tried to pull his hand away but it was no use.

'Listen to me just this once, Lazarus,' Red said, slowly sitting up. Lazarus could see that he was already beginning to heal. Could anything ever really damage him? 'You must go back through the veil and close it. You will be needed on the other side sooner than you think. '

Lazarus struggled against Red's grip. 'What do you mean? Isn't closing the veil enough? That's what I've had to do from the beginning, isn't it? Since Dad put that hole through it?'

Red said, 'Just close it, Lazarus. Go back through and close it now!'

Red then stood and Lazarus felt himself tossed to the side like a small child. He landed roughly on the floor, but sprang up quickly. Why was he going to be needed on the other side so soon? What was Red on about? Lazarus wasn't about to be cast off without knowing exactly what was going on, because he had a horrible feeling that things were now much worse than when this had all started. Much, much worse.

'I need some answers,' said Lazarus, watching as Red stretched and pulled himself back into shape like a wrestler prowling the ring before a fight. His wings were flexing in and out, causing tiny dust devils to dance in the grey light across the floor.

'We all need answers,' said Red. 'Yet do we so rarely ask the right questions?'

'Tell me,' said Lazarus and pointed the spike up towards the hole in the cavern roof. 'Up there, what was going on? Who was that person in white? And what did they do to Dad? I couldn't see; I need to know!'

'There is not enough time to explain,' said Red. 'You must go through now.'

'And why aren't the Dead just swarming through this hole in the veil right now? Why haven't they already started going through?' continued Lazarus. 'What are they waiting for? I mean, someone or something tricked Dad into thinking he could bring Mum back from the dead, just to get him to open up a hole in the veil. Well here it is, right in front of us. So why the wait?'

Red was silent and Lazarus didn't flinch from his stare.

'The Dark is what they have been waiting for, Lazarus,' said Red. 'The Dark.'

'What?'

Red did not reply.

'That's not enough,' said Lazarus. 'The Dark? What are you talking about? Tell me!'

'This wasn't about getting a hole through the veil at all,

was it, Red?' said Craig suddenly.

Red looked from Lazarus to Craig, but he betrayed no emotion, no response.

'What do you mean it wasn't about the hole?' said Lazarus, looking at Craig in confusion. I thought ...'

'This was about your dad,' said Craig, interrupting. 'The Dead didn't need a hole through the veil at all, did they, Red? They needed your dad, Laz. They needed Tobias.'

14
KILLING BLOW

'You're lucky to have a friend such as Craig,' said Red, as Craig's words cemented themselves into Lazarus's mind. 'He has quite an extraordinary ability to see clearly, despite the dirt in the eyes of all humankind. Particularly yours.'

'That sounds more like you,' said Lazarus sarcastically. 'Riddles again. And slightly biblical, too. Well done. I'm almost scared.'

'Not riddles,' said Red. 'Craig?'

Craig look to Red and nodded.

What is it that you can see that Lazarus cannot?'

Craig shrugged. 'I don't know what you mean.'

'Tell me,' said Lazarus. 'Whatever it is, tell me.'

Craig paused, like he was trying to put his thoughts into the right order, then spoke. 'This wasn't about getting a hole through the veil,' he said again. 'The Dead wanted your dad. They needed him for something.'

Craig looked at Red. Red nodded.

'The stuff that we saw rip into him – that's this Dark stuff, isn't it?'

Red nodded again, folded his arms.

'That's why they needed your dad, Laz. Not to put a hole through the veil, but to fill with the Dark stuff. That's what I think anyway. It's the only thing that makes sense. Or like you said, the Dead would be rushing through the hole by now, wouldn't they?'

Lazarus saw Red look over to him. 'A Keeper can open a hole or gateway through the veil from the Living to the Dead, wherever and whenever they see fit.'

'Why?'

'It is rare, but it is generally to send something pretty big back.'

'Like what?' asked Craig.

'Me,' said Red, and didn't give Lazarus or Craig a chance to respond. 'But that is irrelevant now. The Dead have your father, Lazarus. They have someone in their control who has the power to open a new gate from *their* side whenever and wherever they wish.'

Red's words twisted Lazarus's gut. And what was that about something big being sent back, like him? What kind of skeletons was Red hiding in his closet? Lazarus was pretty sure he never wanted to find out. He also had a horrible dread that one day, he would.

'But Dad's dead,' he said, hoping his thoughts weren't playing out loud and clear on his face. 'I saw what happened to him!'

'He would be better off dead,' Red sighed. 'At least he would be at peace. But that matters not. What *does* matter is that you get through the veil now, close this hole, and prepare! It's your only chance.'

'If Dad's still alive,' said Lazarus, 'then take me to him. We need to rescue him!'

'No!' bellowed Red, and with a flick of his wings sent himself across to Lazarus. 'Listen to me, Lazarus! Your only chance to save anyone – including your father – is to go back now!'

'But why?'

'The Dark, Lazarus! It has a terrible power!'

'No kidding!' said Lazarus. 'I saw what it did to Dad! It

bloody well near tore him apart, then vapourised him!'

When Red spoke again, his voice was soft but no less unsettling. 'Imagine, Lazarus, all of humanity's wickedness distilled into something you could use as a weapon. Think of its power, what it could do if used on the Living!'

'You mean Dad's a weapon?'

Red wasn't able to answer as a crash sounded from above and something landed in the centre of the cavern, directly beneath the hole in the roof.

'The Dead are coming, Lazarus,' said Red, turning to the thing unravelling itself on the floor. 'You have to go through now and close the veil behind you!'

'You've not told me enough!' said Lazarus. 'This Dark stuff – what is it? What does it do? How do we stop it? And, for the last time, I don't know how to close the hole in the veil!'

The thing on the floor was almost standing.

'Death opened it, Lazarus,' said Red. 'Death can seal it shut.'

'Enough with the riddles!' yelled Lazarus.

He had barely time to register that the thing was looking at him before Red was on it like a wolf with a lamb.

'I think I get it,' said Craig, and Lazarus knew that whatever Craig was about to say, he really didn't want to hear it.

'Just tell me,' said Lazarus. 'Just get it out, OK?'

In the centre of the cavern, Red was standing over the remains of the thing that had dropped into the cavern. Lazarus saw him look up as three more fell from the roof and landed hard in front of him.

'Someone has to die to close it,' Craig went on. 'Your dad used your mum's ashes to open it, and the car wreck that killed her and nearly killed you. It's all about death. You have to die.'

'Bullshit,' spat Lazarus. 'I've died twice already! And no way in hell, or wherever we are, am I doing it again!'

'Then you must do it, Craig.'

Lazarus and Craig snapped round to see Red facing them, three creatures just away from him and readying for an attack.

'Death is the only way.'

Lazarus saw Craig do a double take. 'You mean kill Lazarus? Kill my mate?'

Red did not reply, but that was answer enough.

'Screw you!' yelled Craig. 'No way am I doing that!'

'There's no time!' shouted Red as the three creatures started to encircle him. 'Do it now! Use the spike!'

Lazarus was suddenly very aware of the weapon in his hand. He stared down at it and looked up at Craig. Was it really the only option? Seriously?

'Don't worry,' said Craig, 'there's no way I'm doing it. No way at all.'

Lazarus only sort of heard him. He was thinking about dying again. Like he'd said, he'd done it twice and had it really been so bad? Had it? He was still here. What if Craig did the thing now, pushed him through? Wouldn't Arielle be able to bring him back? As he looked at Craig he felt the thorns on the handle of the spike retract a little, like they were ready to let go.

One of the creatures let out a cry. It sounded like a bird having its neck wrung. As if this were a signal, a black torrent of the things fell through the hole in the ceiling like water from a burst tap, and the three attacked.

Lazarus and Craig fell back.

'We have to help him,' said Lazarus, pushing back

thoughts of death for a minute, as he watched Red returned the call with a battle cry and flung himself into the spewing throng, with his wings spinning, hurling the creatures into the cavern walls to the awful sound of bones breaking, bodies splitting and bursting. The grey light of the cavern was soon splattered with gore. Red let out a whistle, loud and sharp.

'Sounds like he's calling for his dog,' said Craig.

Lazarus knew what was coming. 'He is,' he said, and pointed.

From the hole in the roof they came. Lazarus couldn't tell how many. Tentacles of thorns, black and damp, spilling and twisting into each other, they fell on to the battle below. It was impossible to see where one of them ended and another began. But he didn't really care. Being at a safe distance from Red's Creatures of Oblivion – his *hounds* – was all that mattered. And the destruction they were now causing was a chaos of screams and dismemberment.

'They're on our side, right?' asked Craig.

'They're on Red's side,' said Lazarus. 'But now we need to get back through the veil.'

Craig was already backing off. 'What Red said, it doesn't make sense,' he spluttered. 'There has to be another way!'

Lazarus could see the confusion and terror in Craig's eyes. It brought tears to his own.

'Look,' he said, 'Arielle's on the other side, right? She'll know what to do – she'll be able to bring me back. She's done it once already!'

'I'm not listening to this . . .'

'You have to!'

'I'm not going to ram that thing into you!' shouted Craig. 'You can't force me to do it – no one can! Not even Red!'

'If you don't do it, then I will!'

Lazarus raised the spike, placed the tip of it against his chest.

'Don't be a bloody idiot!' shouted Craig. 'You can't!'

'I've got no choice!' Lazarus shouted.

Before Lazarus could react, Craig jumped at him and grabbed the spike.

'No,' he said through gritted teeth. 'There's got to be another way! Just . . . let . . . *go!*'

For a few moments Lazarus wrestled with Craig, trying to stop him wrenching the spike away. If he had to die, then so be it. He'd come back like last time. He knew it. Or at least he thought he did.

A flash of bloody rags caught Lazarus's eye. One of the creatures fighting Red had peeled off to make its way over to them. He had only seconds to react before it was on Craig.

With a heave, Lazarus knocked Craig away, sending him to the floor on his back. Using the momentum, he brought the spike round in a swift arc. It caught the creature across its face, cutting deep, and sent it spinning backwards. And before it could do anything to stop itself, it was engulfed by ripping, slime-and-gore-drenched tentacles and pulled to pieces.

But the force of what Lazarus had done had unbalanced him. He tried to stop himself from falling, but it was no good. He toppled down on to Craig, crushing the wind from him.

Neither moved. Lazarus could feel a pain in his arm.

'Laz . . .'

'I . . . I think it got me,' said Lazarus, rolling off Craig.

Blood was pouring from a deep gash. And to one side lay the spike.

'Oh shit, Laz,' said Craig. 'You're hurt . . . your arm!'

'It's OK,' said Laz, but he felt weak, could sense blood freely flowing from him. He was anything but OK.

'Craig!' came Red's voice from across the cavern. 'Do it now! But you need to be in the veil itself! Do it!'

Craig for once looked utterly bemused and lost. The spike was cradled in his hands, bloodied and awful. He was shaking his head, muttering.

Lazarus attempted a smile. 'I'll be fine,' he said. 'Trust me!'

'Craig!' came Red again. 'The coup de grace, Craig! The killing blow! Get him in the veil and do it NOW!'

Craig shook his head even more violently. He allowed the spike to clatter uselessly to the ground.

'I can't do it!' he yelled out. 'No way! I just can't! He's my friend!'

Lazarus felt a wave of relief. But it was short lived as he turned to see Red pull himself from what was left of the battle and approach them, his shoulders low.

When Red was by his side, Lazarus looked up. He

attempted a smile. Red said nothing, just bent down and lifted up Lazarus gently, grabbing the spike and slipped it into Lazarus's belt. Then he turned and walked towards the veil.

'You can't kill him!' shouted Craig, and Lazarus knew this was tearing him apart.

Red stopped. 'What I am about to do,' he said, 'will only buy time. It may make things worse.'

Lazarus was confused. Wasn't Red going to kill him then?

'I am unable to kill the living,' said Red, answering Lazarus's unspoken question. 'Rules, you see? We all have them.'

Lazarus managed to find what was left of his voice. 'What do you mean?' he asked. 'What are you going to do?'

They were at the veil now. It was within an arm's reach.

'I can block the veil, Lazarus. But understand this – it will only be temporary. I cannot stay forever. Without its guardian, Hell will fail if left unchecked for too long, though I fear its walls are already weak.'

Again, Lazarus saw a flicker of something like humanity in Red's face. But it vanished in a second.

Red leant in close. Lazarus could see the blood throbbing in the veins in his eyes.

'Find Abaddon!' Red said. 'Find him and prepare for the Dark!'

With Red's voice still echoing in his head, Lazarus felt himself lifted up and tossed forward like a rag doll. As he flew backwards through the veil he caught sight of Craig following in the same way.

Then darkness snatched him.

15

❧ BURNED ALIVE ❧

Lazarus saw the ground coming too late; he didn't even have time to brace himself and protect his face. He slammed into it hard, felt his breath punched out of his lungs. He coughed, and it felt like his lungs were about to follow through and make a break for freedom. The thought almost made him laugh. But the pain he was in shot that thought dead.

Craig landed next to him with a thud that made Lazarus wince. He couldn't help but think there must be an easier way to get through the veil. One that didn't involve pain and being hit in the face by the ground.

'Lazarus!'

Lazarus raised his head, spat grit. The air was fizzing with a crackle of static, which he guessed was from the veil. But it smelt different, clearer, more clean. This was real normal air, realised Lazarus with relief, even though it was a little stale.

Just away and to the left of him, sitting on the ground and leaning against the cavern wall, was Arielle. And God, did she look a mess. Lazarus remembered the fight with Legion, the demon or whatever the hell it had been, that had damn near torn them all apart.

Arielle's black hair was even more matted than usual, though now it was glued to her head in thick bloody rivulets. She was propping herself up, one raised knee peering through her torn jeans: red, grazed and oozing.

For the first time, Lazarus noticed Arielle's boots. They were black, chisel-toed and leather, and would've looked just fine in an old cowboy movie. They were dust-coloured now though, and scuffed beyond repair. But they were real. They didn't reek of decay. And neither did she. Her thin, white face peered through the strands of her hair, like she was staring through metal railings. Her smile was of relief.

'Arielle,' Lazarus coughed and next to him saw that Craig was just beginning to realise he was in one piece. He felt his head spin and had a job stopping himself from passing out. 'Arielle ... I ...'

Lazarus's world went black and swirly. He heard footsteps dash over to him, felt someone stop his head cracking the ground again. But it couldn't have been Arielle. Or Craig. Who ...?

Lazarus looked up. And the eyes he saw staring back at him sent him cold.

'Clair ...' he breathed, and felt it freeze as it slipped past his lips. He tried to push away from her. Couldn't. Lazarus knew he was back on the right side of the veil all right. But what was she doing here? As undead as she was, seeing her sent a crack of pain through him like a knife wound.

'Don't talk,' said Clair, pushing her brown hair away from her eyes.

Just like Lazarus remembered, Clair looked like a whole world of normal. There was nothing outlandish or peculiar about her at all. She was the kind of girl you'd pass in the street and never be able to remember. Even her clothes reeked of nothing out of the ordinary: jeans and trainers and a hoodie.

Her calm, clear voice made feel Lazarus feel at ease for

a moment. But she was a professional nurse, wasn't she? Making people feel at ease was her job, particularly before she jammed a needle in them. Or a spike.

'You tried to kill me,' he said and felt confused.

He knew it hadn't been Clair who'd attacked him in the hospital where he'd been recovering from being shot by Arielle, but the Dead thing that had slipped into her and taken her over. That didn't make it any easier seeing her here.

'You need to try not to move,' said Clair. 'You're seriously wounded. And what's with the clothes? You look like death! I don't know what I can do . . .'

That grabbed Lazarus's attention. His mind cleared. He remembered the spike ramming into his arm, and with the memory came the pain and the fear. He turned to look at the wound. There was so much blood, it looked like it had been dipped in paint.

Electricity again, a crackle in the air. Lazarus looked back at the veil. The movement made him wince.

'Craig?'

Craig glanced over, nodded. 'What's that sound?'

'The veil,' said Lazarus. 'I think the hole's closing.'

'Red's shut it down?'

'Don't know,' said Lazarus. 'I don't know what he's done.'

The electricity sparked and crackled like fireworks, and an instant later died to nothing, leaving the air to smell of burning and iron. Lazarus stared for a moment at where he and Craig had crossed over. Now all he could see was the car wreck on the other side of the cavern. It wasn't quite so spectacular.

Craig saw Clair.

'What are you doing here? You tried to kill him!'

'I didn't,' replied Clair, not even looking at Craig, busying herself with Lazarus. 'It wasn't me. Look, we haven't got time. Lazarus needs attention.'

'You've given him plenty of that already,' said Craig.

Lazarus was close to spinning out for good here. He had to hold on. If he didn't, he had a feeling he'd be seeing the other side of the veil again, but for all the wrong reasons, and with no chance of coming back. He wasn't about to let himself die.

'Lazarus! Stay with me!'

Lazarus forced himself to look up, saw concern in

Clair's eyes as she glanced over to Arielle. 'I can't do anything about the wound!' she said. 'He's lost too much blood already. He needs an ambulance!'

'Won't come in time,' said Arielle, and Lazarus could hear bubbles in her voice as he watched her push herself off the cavern wall to crawl over.

'No, you can't move,' said Clair, snapping round. 'Your injuries are too serious. Stay still – I'll call for assistance!'

'Won't be any coming,' said Arielle. 'And even if they did, trust me, they wouldn't know what to do.'

Lazarus lay helpless in Clair's arms as Arielle dragged herself painfully across the floor. He could tell that every movement was agony, but she wasn't stopping. He'd seen her fight and wondered if anything could.

'You look like shit,' said Lazarus and enjoyed the whisper of a smile that cracked Arielle's face.

Without any warning, she reached over to the spike and wrenched it from Lazarus's arm. Clair was too slow to stop her and Lazarus wasn't given time to think how she didn't even flinch when she grabbed the handle, how the thorns on it had no effect. A wave of pain engulfed him and he felt Arielle clamp her hands over the wound and squeeze hard. The last words he heard before his world turned to stardust and black were Arielle saying, 'I've seriously got to think about getting a different job.'

And then she screamed.

The sound raced out of her on a stream of light brighter than a star gone supernova. Lazarus was fading in and out of consciousness, but he caught sight of it. It looked like a torch beam strafing the night.

Between the darkness and Arielle's scream, Lazarus felt like he was being burned alive. She seemed to be pulling something from him, and it felt like it was covered in thorns and stuck into him deep. He squirmed instinctively, his body wanting the pain to stop. But Arielle held him fast, like she'd lashed him down. He struggled again, broke free a little, but Clair was on to him in a moment, holding him with her whole body.

The pain eventually pulled Lazarus wide awake. He could see Arielle's hands on the wound, and they – and his arm – were glowing almost white with heat. He could hear a hissing sound, see his blood drying up. The wound, he knew, was healing.

With a final yell, Arielle pulled her hands away and flopped to the ground beside Lazarus. Her breathing was deep and slow, and her eyes were sunk deep. Lazarus had seen some of the Dead in better shape, but he decided to keep that to himself.

Clair dashed over. 'Are you OK? What did you do? What *was* that?'

Lazarus saw Arielle sit up and push Clair away. 'I need to speak to Lazarus and Craig,' she said. 'I'll be fine.'

'You don't look fine,' said Lazarus, his voice barely a whisper. 'You look like how I feel.'

Arielle shrugged. 'Even angels have off days. And I can't remember the last time I had a drink. What happened through the veil?'

'I was dreading you asking me that,' Lazarus said.

'I'm dreading what you're going to tell me.'

And then Lazarus did just that, Arielle not interrupting. He didn't leave anything out. Right from the moment he found himself on the other side of the veil and saw the creature with Craig, through to the house, the meeting with Red, and then – most difficult of all – what they witnessed outside. And his dad.

'Are you sure it was Tobias?'

'Totally,' said Lazarus. 'It was ...' his voice petered out as the images flashed up again in his mind.

'It's OK,' said Clair, resting a hand on Lazarus. 'Don't say if you can't.'

'He must,' said Arielle. 'What else? There was the Dark, your father, crowds. What else? Anything?'

Lazarus shook his head. 'No, that was it,' he said. 'That figure in white just kept slamming the Dark stuff into him and then he was gone. Red didn't do anything, or couldn't. He saved us anyway.'

'There was no clue as to what was going to happen? What the Dead were planning?'

'No,' said Lazarus. 'I've told it as I saw it. It was horrible. I want to forget it, but can't. I just keep reliving what happened to Dad. And knowing he's still alive, trapped there ... I don't know what to do.'

'It's all true,' said Craig. 'He's not missed anything out, trust me. It really was that bad.'

'Red saved you though,' said Arielle, pushing herself to her feet and using her sword as a walking stick. 'He's never one for getting involved. But in this he's been involved from the start.'

'Red threw us back through the veil,' said Lazarus. 'He said something about death being able to close it, tried to get Craig to kill me so it would seal shut as we went through.'

Arielle looked at Craig. 'You should've done as Red told you,' she said. 'I was here. Lazarus was in no danger.'

'Except for being dead,' said Craig. 'I couldn't do it.'

Lazarus looked up at Arielle. 'What's Red done?' he asked. 'The hole in the veil's been blocked, hasn't it? How did he do it?'

A grave look cast itself across Arielle's face like a breeze over water, making her shiver.

'He's used himself to shut it down,' she said. 'Thrown himself into the veil. But he knew if he did that, he was taking a gamble with something much scarier than his own chances of survival.'

'I don't like the sound of that,' said Craig.

'And shouldn't,' said Arielle. 'Hell doesn't exactly come with a pleasant soundtrack.' She turned her head away and muttered under her breath. 'Red, you fool . . .'

She hurled her sword across the cavern. Everyone ducked. When the blade landed it didn't clatter – it burrowed its way into a crack in the wall.

Lazarus waited a few moments before he spoke again. 'I don't understand something,' he said.

'You're not alone,' Craig muttered.

'We've seen the land of the Dead now, and that looks pretty hellish to me.'

Arielle started to walk across the cavern to retrieve her sword.

'So what's Hell?' asked Lazarus. 'How is that any worse?'

Arielle reached up, gripped her sword, and gave it a ferocious tug. The force pulled out not just the sword, but a cascade of rubble that fell around her feet. When she walked back, she was holding the weapon at the ready.

'Red is Hell's gatekeeper,' said Arielle, 'and Hell gives even the Dead nightmares. For even they have the slimmest sense of hope.'

'How?'

'They can change,' she said. 'If they deal with what

they've done, why they're there, they can move on. Most don't though, as I'm sure you saw. They're not interested in redemption.'

'Let me guess,' said Craig. 'Demons are what's in Hell, right?'

'In a way,' said Arielle, 'but those demons are only the playthings of what is really imprisoned there, sent out to slip past Red and cause dismay and destruction.'

'You mean Red can't stop them?' asked Lazarus. He didn't like the sound of where Arielle was going with this.

Arielle shook her head. 'It's like trying to catch smoke. And it's why he has the Creatures of Oblivion. They are always on the hunt. To stop not only the Dead, but the things that slip between the cracks. Without Red to get in the way ... to block the road ...'

'So what's really imprisoned in Hell?' asked Craig. 'Not that I actually want to know.'

'But your curiosity is insatiable.' said Arielle. Then her face grew dark. 'Imagine a creature like me, an angel.' Her voice filled with sorrow and dropped to a whisper. 'Its heart turned black with greed and lust and envy. Think of that power – the power of the beginning of all things – turned to selfishness and evil. That is what resides in Hell. And without Red guarding Hell, without him and the Creatures of Oblivion stalking the land of the Dead, those creatures will now be free. The Dead are coming, Lazarus, but Hell is following ...'

'Well aren't you just the happiness fairy,' said Craig.

Arielle's words flashed something up in Lazarus's mind. 'That's it,' he said. 'Red mentioned something else. I'd totally forgotten it.'

'What?' asked Arielle.

'It was a name,' said Lazarus, wishing he had the strength to push himself away from Arielle and her intense stare. 'Red said we should find them and prepare for the Dark.'

'Who?'

Lazarus squeezed his eyes shut to try and force the name to the front of his mind. But it wasn't clear. He couldn't see it well enough. What was it?'

'Ab something,' he said. 'Abrillon ... Abannon ...'

'Abaddon,' said Arielle. 'He told you to find Abaddon.'

16
🕱🕱 BRUTAL REPUTATION 🕱🕱

Arielle slumped to the floor at Lazarus's feet.

'Oh, Abaddon ... How many years has it been?'

'You say that like it's a bad thing,' said Craig. 'Who is he?'

'An abomination,' said Arielle. 'Abaddon is an abomination.'

Lazarus watched Arielle try to get up again and fail, falling back to the ground with a faint cry. He didn't like her answer, not one bit. 'That doesn't answer Craig's question,' he said. 'Who is he?'

'I'm weak,' said Arielle, her face screwing up in pain. 'Healing you, I thought ... it felt OK. But now, I don't know.'

'You're still avoiding the question.' Lazarus could feel himself getting annoyed. He didn't care how much pain she was in. He wasn't going to be fobbed off. Or dragged somewhere else without knowing what he was getting himself into.

'No, I'm not,' said Arielle, and Lazarus heard her voice falter. 'Every time I heal a Keeper, they take a little of me into them. It drains me. And I've healed you twice in the last few days. I'm amazed I've survived at all.'

'I don't care,' said Lazarus, shocked by how cold he sounded. 'You're an angel so you can't die, can you?'

'Death comes in many shapes ... many sizes,' said Arielle, attempting a smile.

But Lazarus was losing patience. 'You're as bad as Red with your riddles,' he said, unable to hold back the flicker of a sneer. 'Who is Abaddon? Can he help get Dad back?'

He hadn't lost his focus in any of this. It still boiled down to finding his dad. He'd been so close ... He wasn't going to mess up again.

Arielle flickered her eyes to Clair. 'Can you drive?'

Clair nodded and Arielle reached into her jacket and threw her a bunch of keys.

'Then we go.'

Lazarus was on his feet. 'We're not going anywhere until you answer me!' He didn't like being ignored and could feel his strength racing back like hot lead through his veins, firing through him. He felt indestructible. 'Who is Abaddon? Why's he so important?'

'You'll meet him soon enough,' said Arielle. 'And then he can tell you himself. Assuming of course that he doesn't kill us all on sight.'

'And why would he do that?'

'We have a history,' said Arielle. 'We've not always been on the same side.'

Lazarus saw a dark glint spark in her eye.

'Then why would Red send us to him?' he asked.

'It certainly wasn't as a joke,' said Arielle, 'though I don't doubt that even now he's having a little laugh to himself about it. Ever the fool.'

'Can't say he struck me as a hugely funny guy,' said Craig. 'He's hardly a laugh a minute, is he?'

'You're not making sense, Arielle,' said Lazarus. 'Again.'

Arielle rested her hand on Lazarus's chest, directly over his heart. It seemed to respond, thumping faster for a moment.

'You have to trust me,' she said. 'I can't tell you anymore. Not yet. There's no time. We need to get on the road now. No hesitation. We've quite a journey ahead, OK?'

Lazarus made to complain, but Arielle's stare held him back.

'OK,' he nodded. 'Let's go. But I still want answers.'

Lazarus pushed himself to his feet, then helped Craig up. A few moments ago, he'd felt like every bit of his body was broken or bruised. It hadn't been the kind of pain he'd had at school from the occasional playground fight or rugby scrum; more like he'd been locked in a room with a gorilla armed with a baseball bat. But that pain had faded. And now standing up, it seemed to have gone completely, no aches, nothing. Which didn't make sense.

'Don't take this the wrong way,' said Craig, looking Lazarus up and down and breaking his train of thought, 'but you look like crap.'

'Thanks for pointing out the obvious,' replied Lazarus.

'I'm your mate, that's my job.'

'I actually feel fine, though. I mean seriously fine. No pain, no aches, nothing. How weird's that?'

Then Lazarus glanced at Craig and if he looked bad, then Craig looked a whole lot worse. He was still covered in Red's blood, but in patches his skin was white with dust. His clothes were unrecognisable. He looked like the very definition of a nightmare.

'You know *you* look worse, right?'

Craig shrugged. 'At least I'm not the one who keeps getting stabbed and killed. You should be more careful. Or this'll be the death of you.'

Lazarus grinned. He was struck then by just what a friend Craig was. He'd been dragged into this by accident. If Lazarus hadn't phoned him for help at the hospital, he'd have been out of it utterly. He certainly wouldn't have been to the land of the Dead and back. But here he was, and still cracking jokes. Unbelievable.

'Clair?'

'Yeah?'

'How are we going to do this? You're the one with the medical background. Tell us.'

'We need to get her somewhere we can lie her down,'

Clair replied. 'I don't know what else I can do except monitor her condition. I've never, you know, dealt with someone like her. If you know what I mean.'

'You mean an angel?'

Clair nodded. 'I've no idea about her physiology, what treatments she can take, what her normal heart rate is. For God's sake, she shouldn't even exist! I feel like a first year student who's been sent to a car crash in their first week!'

'We'll just have to do the best we can,' said Lazarus. 'Arielle?'

Arielle raised her head, peeled her eyes back. 'Yes?'

'Can you walk?'

'If I've someone to lean on, yes,' she replied. 'I'm sorry, this is my fault. I didn't take into account everything I'd gone through before healing you again, Lazarus.'

'You mean you might not have done it if you'd thought about it?'

'No,' Arielle smiled. 'But I might've thought twice before walking around so soon afterwards and launching my sword into the air.'

'That was pretty impressive,' said Lazarus.

'Actually,' said Clair, grabbing his wrist and feeling his pulse, 'so is your recovery. How do you feel?'

'The wound in my arm's healed up and all my aches seem to have gone,' Lazarus said. He looked down at Arielle. 'You know that whole smell of death thing, and how it can affect Keepers, send us all woozy and make us want to hurl?'

'Yes,' said Arielle. 'You will get used to it, I promise.'

'Already have,' said Lazarus. 'I still feel it, but I can control it now. It's like I can lock it away into a little room in my head where I can see myself being sick if I peer through the door, but so long as I stay out of the room, I feel fine.'

'And you really don't feel even an ache from that wound? Or tired at all?'

'I should, I know,' said Lazarus. 'But I don't. I feel good. Better than good actually.'

Arielle looked at him like she was confused.

'What's wrong?'

'I've healed you twice now,' said Arielle. 'And Red had his hand on you a long time ago.'

'Exactly,' said Lazarus. 'And I feel fine. You don't

need to sound all concerned. You're the one really hurt so let's get going, OK?'

'But I *am* concerned, Lazarus,' said Arielle. 'Your ability to heal has obviously been affected because of what's happened. Your recovery period is shortening. It's like you're ... no, that's impossible.'

Arielle's voice drifted to nothing.

'What's impossible?' asked Lazarus.

'I don't know of any Keeper who could do what you can do,' said Arielle. 'Your dad was good at his job, but that was it. He was still human. But you ...'

'Just get to the point,' said Lazarus, growing impatient.

'She means,' said Craig, 'that whatever power Arielle and Red have has affected you. Look at your amazing recovery period. You should really be down on the floor with Arielle feeling as crap as you still look – yeah, you're in serious need of a shower, Laz. But instead, you're up on your feet feeling great. Considering what you've been through, you look better than ever, and that's with those clothes on and all that blood.'

Lazarus knew they had a point. 'But so what if I heal

quicker? That's a good thing, surely!'

'Who can say, Lazarus?' said Arielle. 'Whichever way you look at it, it's pretty extraordinary. Now, shall we go and find Abaddon?'

With nothing else to add, particularly because he couldn't understand why anyone would be worried about him feeling *better*, Lazarus helped Craig lift Arielle up from the floor. She weighed nothing. Lazarus wasn't surprised. She looked so thin he wondered if she ever broke by simply sneezing.

As they walked across the cavern, Lazarus asked, 'Where can we find this Abaddon, then?'

'That's a good question,' said Arielle. 'Usually he finds you. But you'd better hope he doesn't. His reputation is somewhat unique.'

'How do you mean?'

'Brutal,' said Arielle. 'He has his own methods, and as effective as they are, that doesn't make them right.'

'So how do we find him?'

'We go to where he now rests,' said Arielle. 'Though I'm only assuming he's still there, after all these years.'

'Still where?' asked Lazarus. 'How many years is

it since you saw him?'

'I find it easier to talk in terms of centuries,' said Arielle.

'How many?'

'Nearly three.'

'But Red spoke of him as though he was alive!' said Lazarus. 'Three hundred years?'

'Little has been heard of Abaddon for nearly four hundred years,' she said. 'He has kept himself well hidden, and with good reason – there are many who would try to destroy him. Few know where he now rests.'

'You make it sound like he's dead,' said Craig.

Arielle's face didn't flicker. 'That's because he is.'

17
RUINED ETERNITY

Arielle's eyes glazed over and her legs buckled. Craig, and Lazarus caught her before she piled into the floor. 'That was close,' said Lazarus and looked over to Clair. 'Is she OK? What happened?'

'She's passed out,' Clair replied, kneeling down to examine Arielle. 'Out cold I'd say. We need to get her to her vehicle as quick as we can. At least then she'll be comfortable.'

'Have you seen it?' asked Craig. 'I don't think it was designed for comfort. Knocking buildings down maybe. Or destroying mountains. But not comfort.'

'Doesn't matter,' said Clair. 'She told me she basically lives in it. It can't be any worse than your average ambulance. I've had some hellish rides in those, I can tell you.'

'The only difference is the number of wine bottles on the floor,' said Lazarus.

'How do you mean?' asked Clair.

'Arielle likes to drink,' said Lazarus.

'But she's an angel,' said Clair. 'I didn't think, well, you know . . .'

'No, I do,' said Lazarus. 'I was surprised as well. But when I first met her and saw the bottle of wine in her hand, I was more bothered about her sword. That was just a couple of minutes before she put a bullet in me.'

'Why does she drink?'

Lazarus shrugged. 'I'm guessing she's seen some stuff that anyone would want to drown out, right?'

'I guess,' said Clair.

'Come on,' Lazarus said to Craig. 'Let's get up there before she wakes up and has a go at us.'

Lazarus was again struck by how light Arielle was. And now she wasn't even helping and they were doing their best to keep her feet from dragging across the floor. It felt like they were carrying a child she was so light. But he'd seen her fight, knew just how strong she was. Arielle, Lazarus realised, was a puzzle he'd never solve. There was stuff in her head that he was happy for her to keep there. Whatever had turned her into this ... well, he hoped he didn't meet it in a dark alleyway.

Halfway up the steps out of the cavern, Lazarus asked Clair to take over his side of Arielle before heading back down.

'Where's he going?' Clair said.

'No idea,' said Craig. 'He's been acting kind of weird. Keeps saying he can see dead people. I keep telling him to stop quoting the only good movie with Bruce Willis in it.'

'You don't like Bruce Willis?'

Craig didn't answer as Lazarus reappeared.

'Where did you go?'

'Forgot these,' said Lazarus, and lifted his hands. One held Arielle's sword. The other held the spike.

'I ... I recognise that,' said Clair, seeing the spike. Then she noticed the thorns sticking through the back of Lazarus's hand. 'But there's no blood!' she gasped. 'That's not possible! Those things, they go right through!'

'Pretty cool, huh?' said Lazarus, and regretted it instantly. It made him sound like he was coming on to

Clair. Nothing was further from his mind. Except perhaps coming on to Craig.

'Makes a pretty effective weapon,' he said and he raised his fist, clenched it. Close up, it looked worse than he realised. The metal thorns were menacing and long, and stained a black-red. And they didn't just protrude through the back of his hand, but through his fingers too. It was nasty and vicious and he had already seen the damage it could cause. For a second, he was shocked by his own actions – that he'd used it not just on the Dead, but on Red . . .

'It doesn't hurt?'

Lazarus could see Clair wasn't convinced, but that was understandable.

'No,' he said, 'and the thorn things are longer now than when you first used this on me.'

'That's why I recognised it,' said Clair. 'I'm so sorry, Laz, I had no idea what . . .'

Her voice broke.

'Doesn't matter now,' said Lazarus. 'Seriously. And it's a pretty cool weapon, all things considered, so really I should say thank you – it's saved my life a few times already.'

'I think you'll find that was me,' said Craig. 'Now, about getting Arielle back to that thing she calls home . . .'

They set off again. In the next cavern, Lazarus clocked the broken coffins against the wall, the ones from which he'd stolen clothes as a disguise for the land of the Dead. And it had worked. Then they were in his dad's workshop. and heading back up the final flight of steps to the house.

'Let's get to the kitchen,' he said, 'grab what we can, then get to Arielle's vehicle.'

Craig said, 'A change of clothes might be a good idea.'

Lazarus agreed, but as they stepped out into the hallway, a thought crossed his mind. Without a word, he turned and headed back into the workshop. He returned with a couple of bottles of wine in each hand from his dad's collection.

'Bit young for the hard stuff, aren't you?' said Clair.

'Figured Arielle might need a little something to help her recover,' said Lazarus.

'Most people prefer medicine to alcohol.'

'Most people aren't angels,' Lazarus replied. 'And we need her not just well, but in a good mood. Or finding Abaddon is going to be a lot harder than we think.'

* * *

It took seven minutes to pack all the food that was worth taking from the kitchen into bags kept under the sink and a further five for him and Craig to scrub themselves as clean as they could, and get changed. And to Lazarus, each of those minutes felt more real than anything he'd ever experienced in his life. After the land of the Dead, to be back in the real world where he'd been born and lived and breathed was like being born again. Everything felt, smelt, tasted fresh and new, like he could sense the potential of the day ahead slipping out of the earth. Colours screamed out at him to be noticed. Just the simple taste of a cool glass of water slipping down his throat lit sparks in his brain. Clean jeans and a T-shirt not caked in mud felt like clothes of a king against his skin. It was as though the whole world was yelling at him to be noticed, to understand just how astonishing it was to be alive in the first place. And just how fragile it all truly was.

'You really don't do anything other than black, do you?' said Craig, his hair a tangled mess, but the rest of him at least looking presentable. 'And I've never even heard of the band this T-shirt seems to belong to.'

Lazarus smiled, enjoying seeing Craig dressed at least almost cool as Clair grabbed her bag from the hall. They headed for Arielle's Defender.

Clair said, 'I dropped it there when I came looking for you. After seeing you race out of the hospital with Arielle chasing. I had to make sure you were OK.'

'I've been meaning to ask about that,' said Lazarus as they slipped out of the front door. 'It was a shock seeing you there.'

'I know, I'm sorry,' said Clair, but Lazarus couldn't help think she sounded like she wasn't telling him everything.

They turned round the back of the house. Out of the shadows the Defender reared its ugly head.

'You didn't just come to check up on us, did you?' said Lazarus as Clair fiddled with the keys to get the vehicle open.

'How do you mean?' replied Clair, not turning to face Lazarus.

'There's more to it than that,' Lazarus said. 'You're not telling me everything.'

Clair stayed silent. Lazarus went to speak, but she pulled the door open and peered inside.

'Nice,' she said.

Lazarus caught a movement out of the corner of his eye. He didn't think about what he did next, just grabbed Clair and pushed her to the ground. The next thing they all heard was the sound of smashing glass.

'Lazarus, what the hell—'

But Lazarus was up on his feet, looking for what he'd seen coming towards them. Then he spotted it: a brick, lying among freshly smashed bottles in the back of the Defender. He reached in and pulled it out.

'What is it?' asked Craig, peering in, now taking most of Arielle's weight.

'There's a note on it.' Lazarus picked up the brick.

'You sure you want to touch that?' asked Clair. 'It's covered—'

'In blood, I know,' said Lazarus. But he'd seen plenty of that this past few days. A little bit extra made no difference.

The note stuck to his fingers as he unravelled it, the blood not quite wet, not quite dry. He saw his name.

'It's to you then,' said Craig. 'First-class post isn't what it used to be.'

'It's not a note,' said Lazarus. 'It's a photograph. Look.'

He flipped it over to show Clair and Craig.

'That's you,' said Craig, 'but someone's seriously gone to town on your face with a black biro.'

Lazarus wanted to drop the picture, stamp on it, anything. It suddenly felt very wrong to have it in his hands, like it was contaminated with something unseen.

'Who sent it?' asked Clair.

Lazarus shrugged. 'There's no writing on it,' he said. 'It's just a scribbled mess.'

A hand shot out, grabbed the photograph, screwed it up and dropped it to the ground. Lazarus looked over to see Arielle, stirring now as she leaned against Craig.

'Doesn't matter who sent it,' she said, staring at Lazarus, her voice little more than a dry croak that sounded like splintering wood. 'Let's just get moving.'

Lazarus didn't move. 'It *does* matter,' he said. 'I thought I was just dealing with the Dead. So who threw this? How did they get this picture? Who the hell else knows about what's been going on?'

Arielle's head slumped forward. 'We must move ...'

'Maybe it's a warning,' said Craig.

'Who threw it?' Lazarus demanded. 'Tell me, Arielle!'

Arielle raised her head again. 'Clair, we need to get on the road ...'

'We're not moving until you give me an answer!'

'I'm with Arielle,' said Craig. 'At least if we get on the road we'll be a moving target.'

Lazarus leaned in close to Arielle. 'I'm waiting.'

Arielle raised her eyes to Lazarus. In them he saw such a cold darkness he wanted to pull away.

'The Dead whisper to people, Lazarus,' she said. 'Most don't hear. But some ... those who listen ... they are promised more than just knowledge of life after death.'

'Look,' said Craig, 'I've seen the land of the Dead. It's not that great a place. So what's to promise? Eternity in a world all smashed and broken?'

'The Dead want to return *here*,' said Arielle, 'not stay where they are. This world could provide more than you could ever possibly imagine to a sick mind and a depraved soul. And that's the only kind of ruined eternity some people are interested in.'

'Lunatics,' said Clair.

Arielle shook her head. 'You'd be horribly surprised how sane many of those are who try to help the Dead return.'

Lazarus dropped down and picked up the photograph.

'So it's not just the Dead who want to kill us,' he said, 'but the living too. But why not just do it? Why throw this?'

'They know who you are,' said Arielle. 'Think of it like a game of chess. They're the pawns and you're the most valuable, powerful piece on the board.'

Craig winked at Lazarus. 'Always said you were a bit of a queen.'

'They're not going to take you on,' said Arielle. 'They know they wouldn't stand a chance. But what they will try and do is taunt you and push you into making a wrong move.'

Lazarus stood back up. 'You're really not here to make me feel better, are you?'

'No,' said Arielle. 'I'm here to make sure you stay alive. Now get into the truck and let's get moving!'

18
TWISTED DREAMS

'Where can I put all these bottles?' asked Clair. 'We need to get rid of them if we're to travel in this thing. They're dangerous as much as anything else.'

'Allow me to demonstrate,' said Lazarus and picked up a bottle. He threw it into an area of weeds and scrub. They all heard it smash.

'Not exactly eco,' said Craig.

'I'm saving the world in my own unique way,' said Lazarus. 'Someone else can deal with the recycling.'

It didn't take long to get rid of the rest. Lazarus packed away all the food into the many cupboards and cubbyholes that seemed to just grow out of the inside of the Defender, and they laid Arielle on the narrow single bed along one side. Clair sat beside her, pulled up her bag and opened it.

'You carry that stuff with you all the time?' asked Craig, peering inside at the medical kit.

'I'm a nurse,' said Clair. 'We take our work home.'

'Good job you're not a mortician,' said Craig.

Arielle was drifting in and out of unconsciousness.

'You need to rest,' said Clair.

Arielle pointed to a road atlas strapped to the roof of the Defender, and Clair pulled it down. Arielle flicked through, then dropped a finger on a page. Craig leaned in for a look.

'You're kidding me,' he said. 'That's bloody miles away!'

'The Brock Stone,' said Arielle, her voice fading like the volume was being slowly turned down on a stereo. 'Kentmere. It's in the Lake District. Beautiful place to hide something so terrible. It's where we'll find Abaddon.'

Her eyes rolled shut.

'Where's that, then?' asked Clair.

'What, the Lake District?' said Lazarus. 'You serious? You don't actually know?'

'Look, I've never been further north than Bristol, so you'll have to help me out.'

'North,' said Craig. 'That's all you need to know if you're driving: it's north. Head for the M5 and stay on it until we say to get off.'

Lazarus tossed them both a can of Coke. He had a few more bags of food to squirrel away, but he was thirsty and guessed Clair and Craig were too. And they needed their energy if they were travelling that far north. It would be a five-hour journey at least, and that didn't even take into account toilet breaks. He took a glug, then shuffled up by Clair. 'So, tell me nurse, what do we do with an injured angel who can't stay awake?'

'It's not funny,' said Clair. 'I'm doing something no one else has ever done! It's not like I've read papers on Angel Care!'

He looked down at Arielle. She wasn't unconscious as such, but she was breathing hard, and breaking into a hell of a sweat. When he spoke again, his voice was more serious. 'Is she bad?'

'She's not just burning up,' said Clair, 'she's almost on fire! My thermometer goes to one hundred and ten degrees Celsius, and she's gone way beyond that. If this was you or me, we'd be dead, you understand me? But her heart rate is fine. It doesn't make sense, Laz.'

'Just do the best you can,' Lazarus replied. 'Even if that is just wait. But I'm guessing an angel's body deals with stuff slightly differently than ours.'

'We should take her to a hospital,' said Clair.

Lazarus raised an eyebrow involuntarily. 'And they have a better understanding of angels in hospitals, do they?'

'That's not what I meant.'

'I know. But we have to do as she said. And she was pretty clear back in the cavern that she didn't want any medical attention outside of us providing it.'

Clair closed her bag, rattled the Defender's keys in her hands.

'I've never driven anything this big.'

'We've never driven,' said Craig. 'You win by default.'

Clair clambered over to the driver's seat and Lazarus heard the swish and click of the seatbelt.

'Comfy?'

'I don't know where the key goes,' Clair said. 'I feel like I'm driving a truck.'

'Over there,' Craig pointed.

Clair slipped the key into the ignition and twisted it. The engine roared to life. It sounded like it was clawing every roar and throb from the world outside, sucking in energy and spitting it out again in flames. Lazarus then joined her in the front, slipping over to the passenger seat.

'Whatever engine Arielle's got under that bonnet, I'm guessing it's not general issue.'

'What do you mean?' asked Clair.

'I mean,' said Lazarus, 'just be careful with the throttle. This may look like a posh tank, but it probably shifts like a Porsche.'

'Are you suggesting I can't drive?'

Lazarus shook his head, noticed the look of affront on Clair's face. He had to hide his smile.

'Good,' said Clair.

She slipped the vehicle into reverse, pulled it round and drove it smoothly out on to the road.

As soon as the Defender had pushed its way on to the road, its occupants fell silent. Craig wasted no time in getting his head down and was soon snoring. It was a pleasant sound, Lazarus thought, and laughed to himself.

Usually if Craig stayed over, Lazarus would end up throwing stuff at him to shut him up. But after all the screaming and yelling they'd just come through, it was a welcome change.

Glancing over at Clair, Lazarus saw quiet determination in her eyes. She was completely focused on the road ahead. So he just left her to it, leant over to the stereo and switched it on. The music that slipped quietly into the cabin wasn't what he was expecting – though, if he was honest, an angel's taste in music wasn't something he'd ever really put his mind to. It was country. Something he never listened to in his life. But now, as he rested his head against the cool of the window and gazed out into the normal world on the other side, it seemed to fit. And soon, as the music mingled with the rain starting to fleck the windscreen, and as the skies darkened above, Lazarus allowed his eyes to close. He didn't even dream.

Lazarus woke to the sound of thunder.

'It was too much to expect for it to stay clear,' said Clair as Lazarus rubbed sleep from his eyes.

He felt the Defender accelerate and Clair pulled out

past a slow-moving truck, the power pushing Lazarus back into his seat. Like he'd guessed, Arielle's truck wasn't exactly an everyday run-about. That kind of acceleration didn't come as standard.

The drizzle Lazarus had fallen asleep to was now a downpour and the black clouds above were like thick slabs of tarmac. They looked like they could, at any moment, just fall and squash everything beneath them. Craig shuffled forward.

'Arielle OK?' Lazarus asked, twisting round to look at the sleeping angel.

'Hasn't stirred,' said Craig, 'but that's not what I've come to talk about.'

'Sounds important,' said Lazarus.

'You could say that,' said Craig. 'I've just realised something – Mum hasn't got a clue where I am.'

'Yes she has,' said Lazarus. 'She knows you're with me.'

'She doesn't know when I'll be back though, does she? In fact, I'm sure I said I'd be back today! Crap.'

'What's your mum like?' asked Clair, not moving her eyes from the road ahead.

'Like a hippy,' said Craig. 'Obsessed with tie-dyeing everything and cooking only with stuff that's certifiably organic and based on lentils.'

'Sounds cool.'

'She is,' said Craig. 'Don't know what she'd make of all this though.'

Lazarus handed his phone to Craig. 'Use mine to call her, that way she'll know you're definitely with me and not spinning her a load of guff. Say you're just going to stay round mine for a few more days. It's the holidays, remember? It's not like we've got anywhere to go. And she's always cool about it, so I doubt this time willl be any different.'

'How long have you two known each other?' asked Clair as Craig chatted to his mum.

'Since pre-school,' said Lazarus. 'Craig turned up wearing a werewolf mask.'

'Seriously?'

Lazarus nodded. 'We were three years old, and there's this loon in a horror mask sitting with us like it was just a normal thing to do.'

'Different,' said Clair.

'He was watching Vincent Price when he was seven. His favourite movie at primary was *City of the Dead* starring Christopher Lee. He's obsessed.'

'Cheers,' Craig said, handing the phone back to Lazarus. 'Mum's fine.'

Lazarus could hear a strain in his voice. 'You all right?'

'Headache again,' said Craig. 'Like those ones I had earlier. And I feel a bit sick. Think I'll just lie down for a minute. If it's good enough for an angel, it's good enough for me.'

Lazarus watched his friend lie down, then turned back to Clair.

'He's been getting headaches since we crossed the veil,' he said. 'I don't like it.'

'Have a look through my bag,' said Clair. 'I've some headache tablets in there. They look like horse tablets – huge pink things. They'll knock him out for a while, but he'll wake up a little happier and certainly more rested.'

Craig took the pills without complaint, leant back and closed his eyes. Satisfied, Lazarus went back to gazing through the window at the world outside. In the dull, almost gloopy light, everything looked washed out and grey, and was rushing past chased by the wind and the rain. The roads were rammed, traffic snaking ahead, breaking up now and again to overtake and change lanes, then coming together again. Lazarus found himself staring at the people on their way to wherever they were going. It was like watching a thousand low-budget silent movies all playing at once. In each car and truck and van, a mini-drama was unfolding, but without subtitles Lazarus could only guess what. And strangely, for a moment, he felt desperate to understand, like the lives of everyone beyond where he was sitting were of enormous importance. Their everydays, their nine-to-fives, their early mornings, late nights. Lazarus felt jealous of it all, couldn't help it. Normality felt so far away now. He had no idea if he would ever get it back.

'Do you remember attacking me?'

Lazarus wasn't sure why he asked the question – it kind of just popped out to break the silence.

'No,' said Clair, leaning forward to flick on the radio. 'Well, not like a proper memory. It's more flashes of something I saw happen, like bits of a movie or something.'

'I remember every bit of it,' said Lazarus. 'I was lucky to escape at all. You did some really weird stuff, you know that, don't you?'

Clair just nodded, said nothing.

'So why are you here?' Lazarus didn't understand why Clair was tagging along. He was the Keeper so he had no choice. Craig was his best mate and the only way to stop him coming along would be to kill him. But Clair?

Clair didn't answer. Lazarus didn't like the silence. Too much of it and he'd be thinking about what happened to his dad again. 'It's not like you need to be,' he added.

'Yes I do,' said Clair.

That wasn't a good enough reason for Lazarus so he pushed for more. When Clair started to explain, he could tell that she was finding it difficult. 'When that thing took me over,' she said, her eyes not straying from the road ahead, 'I was helpless. I knew I was going to die, but not then. Not for a long, long time if it had succeeded.'

'That doesn't make any sense.'

'Yes it does,' said Clair, wiping a tear from her cheek. 'When the Dead get into you, they keep you there, but it's like you've been pushed into the corner of a room: I could see what my body was doing, but I wasn't in control of it. And the Dead's thoughts mingled with mine: horrible, twisted dreams.'

'That still doesn't explain why you're here.'

Clair allowed her stare to leave the road ahead for a few seconds and she faced Lazarus. Her stare was of cold stone on a mountain blasted by a winter's storm. 'If you saw how the world was going to end, would you do nothing, or would you do something? Well, I'm doing something. I don't know what, but this is it. It's all I've got.'

Lazarus understood. How could he not? But something else bothered him now. 'So where did you get the spike?' he asked. 'Did someone give it to you?'

'I can't remember.'

'I mean it's a seriously crazy weapon if you think about it. But for you to have it at all – how?'

'Like I said, I can't remember,' said Clair.

Lazarus's frustration seemed to rise much more quickly now, as did his anger. It was difficult to control.

'But you must!' He knew he was raising his voice. 'It's not like it was just a knife or something, is it? It's a weapon from God knows where, and you can't remember anything about how you got it?'

'Don't push it,' snapped Clair.

'Just tell me!' Lazarus yelled and lashed out at the dashboard with his fist. He hit it hard and heard a click, like something had just fallen open. He reached under the dashboard and felt around.

'Lazarus . . .' said Clair.

'Shush,' said Lazarus.

'Look, I'm only saying that . . .'

But Clair didn't finish. Because, from beneath the dashboard, Lazarus removed a long box of grey wood. The grain shone through and it was smooth as glass.

'What's that?' asked Clair.

'It fell out when I hit the dashboard,' Lazarus answered. 'It's a box.'

'Then put it back!' hissed Clair, looking nervously from Lazarus to Arielle. 'Who knows what it could be!'

But Lazarus wasn't listening. He'd found the latch, and with a flick it eased open silently, and what stared up from inside it made him shudder.

19

SAVAGE WEAPONS

'Pretty, isn't it?'

Lazarus was suddenly very aware of a face next to his own and the smell of warm breath coated in a slick of wine. A hand reached past him for the box as Arielle leaned over, her eyes wide and dancing, a corkscrew in her other hand.

Lazarus couldn't stop himself staring at the thing inside the box. It was a spike, just like the one he had himself; just like the one Clair had used to try and kill him. It was identical. And here it was, in a nice little box, all lovely and clean and shiny, and in the vehicle owned by an angel who was apparently there to protect him.

Lazarus was then struck by how much better Arielle looked already. Being an angel obviously had its advantages when it came to recovery. 'It is a weapon from another time, Lazarus,' she said. 'Another world even.'

'It's just like mine,' Lazarus mumbled. 'What's going on?'

'Nothing is going on, Lazarus,' said Arielle. 'It's not exactly unusual for an angel to carry savage weapons like this.'

'And the wine?' asked Clair. 'Seriously, Arielle ...'

'It's the only medicine that works.'

'But what if Clair has to stop driving?' asked Lazarus. 'You're the only other person here who can take over.'

'I'll teach you.'

'Some other time,' said Lazarus. 'Until then, put the cork back in. Now.'

Clair flashed a look at him. He was surprised by how in charge he felt, particularly with Arielle. What was being a Keeper doing to him?

Arielle pushed the cork back in and rested the wine bottle back on a shelf.

'Why do you drink so much?' asked Lazarus. 'I didn't really expect that of someone like you.'

Arielle shuffled herself till she was more comfortable. 'Sometimes Laz,' she said, 'it's the only thing that gets me to sleep. Other times, it's the only thing that'll keep me awake.'

'That's messed up.'

'Being an angel is all about being messed up.'

Lazarus couldn't be bothered to have a deep philosophical discussion, so he changed the subject back to the spike.

'This is yours then?' he said, holding up the box.

Arielle said 'Yes' and reached into the box to pull out the spike. The thorns on the handle slipped into her own hand easily, and pierced the back of her skin without spilling a drop of blood. Neither did she yell out.

'But you don't have the holes like me,' said Lazarus, looking at his own hand and the scars and holes that now covered it. 'Mine are always there now. Where are yours?'

'Have the thing long enough,' said Arielle, 'and you will heal. But the body never forgets, and allows the thing to become a part of it. Quite beautiful, isn't it?'

Arielle raised the spike. The light from outside, speckled by the rain on the windscreen, danced and swirled in tiny whirlpools across the metal.

'So it's an angelic weapon?'

Arielle nodded and rested the spike back in its box. 'That Clair had one showed just how dangerous the Dead believe you to be,' she said. 'As soon as Tobias had crossed over, they wanted you out of the picture.'

'Why?'

'They needed the line of Keepers to end with your father, for him to be the last. And they wanted the last Keeper for themselves.'

Lazarus looked at the spike again. 'That doesn't explain how Clair got hold of one of those,' he said.

'They were made for and by angels,' said Arielle, 'but weapons disappear, Lazarus. Battlefields are treasure troves for anyone interested in finding out how the killing is done. Others find them. Others use them.'

'But who gave it to Clair?'

'No one gave it to me,' said Clair at last. 'I found it. Or at least the thing inside me did. It knew where it was.'

Lazarus didn't like the sound of that and imagined droves of the Dead being armed with these things. If one of them knew how to find such a spike, who was to say others wouldn't be able to do the same?

'Do you remember where it was?' asked Lazarus.

Clair shook her head. 'That thing took me over. I felt like I was trapped, locked in a little room inside myself. I could see things happening, but had no control.'

'So nothing about this, then?' said Lazarus, and pulled out his own spike. It felt good in his hand, like it belonged.

'No,' said Clair. 'If I saw anything, it was what the thing had already seen. It was . . . horrid.'

Arielle rested a hand on Clair's shoulder. 'What did you see?'

'I don't know,' said Clair. 'Fragments of stuff really, like bits of pictures that have been sliced to pieces. It made no sense.'

'Can you remember anything? It might be important.'

'No,' said Clair. 'Nothing. I just saw the Dead. That was it. Thousands of them.'

'What were they doing?'

Clair overtook a car in front. Then she pulled back into the lane and slowed right down. The car she'd overtaken flashed its lights then skipped past. Clair clearly had something else on her mind.

'Everything was burning.' Her eyes stared forward, like they were looking beyond what was on the other side of the windshield. 'And the Dead were all standing still, waiting for something.'

'What were they waiting for, Clair? Tell me.'

Lazarus heard urgency in Arielle's voice. What was she after? What was bothering her?

'I . . . I can't,' said Clair, and Lazarus could see tears forming in her eyes. 'They were waiting, that's all I could sense. And something terrible was coming. They were afraid, helpless. I don't know. I don't know!'

Arielle went to question again, but Lazarus stopped her.

'If she remembers more, she'll tell us,' he said. 'Now let her drive, OK?'

'Lazarus,' said Arielle, 'Clair could have valuable information. We need to—'

'We need to get to Abaddon,' Lazarus cut in. 'That's what we need to do.'

Arielle sat back and Lazarus could tell she wasn't happy.

'You look better,' he said, changing the subject to

take the pressure off Clair. 'Thought you were going to croak on us.'

'It's not that easy to get rid of me.' Arielle smiled, but there was little feeling in it. 'Angels regenerate very quickly compared to most humans.'

'Most?'

'You're not most humans,' said Arielle.

Clair interrupted. 'Someone's following us.'

Arielle snapped round and shuffled down the back of the Defender to get a better look through the rear window.

'How do you know? Which car is it?'

'That black one on the right, two cars down,' said Clair. 'I thought I was making it up, but I was sure I saw it pull out when we left town. Didn't think anything of it as it disappeared. But it's been with us now for the past twenty minutes. I've given it plenty of opportunities to overtake. It hasn't budged.'

'That explains your last manoeuvre,' said Lazarus. 'Thought you were going nuts for a minute – overtaking, then decelerating.'

'What's happening?'

Lazarus glanced into the back of the Defender. Craig was awake.

'Clair thinks we're being followed,' said Lazarus. 'Pleasant dreams?'

Craig pushed a hand through his hair and stretched, bracing his hands on the roof of the Defender. He looked at Lazarus, went to say something, but then his face went white and he yelled out, grabbing his head like he was trying to stop it bursting. Arielle caught him as he toppled forward. For a few moments he lay in her lap, shaking.

Lazarus went to unclip his seat belt and climb over to his friend, but Arielle stopped him.

'He's OK,' she said. 'Let me speak to him.'

'But what the hell was that?' asked Lazarus. 'What happened?'

He'd completely forgotten Craig's headaches. They'd come on after that thing on the other side of the veil had almost had him. Then they'd just disappeared.

Arielle helped Craig sit up again. His face was ash-pale and sweating.

'Craig . . .'

Craig shook his head. 'No ... don't make me remember ...'

'Is he all right?' asked Clair. 'Do I need to look at him?'

'Craig,' said Arielle again. 'What happened?'

'I saw houses,' he said, his voice shaking like a little boy reliving the worst nightmare he'd ever had. 'I don't know if it was a town or village or what ... it was burning, but none of the buildings were damaged. And there was this huge hole or blackness or something. The Dead ... were coming through it.'

Craig's voice dropped.

'What else?' asked Arielle. 'Tell me.'

'There were people,' Craig whispered. 'Adults ... children ... And then the Dead came ...'

'What happened, Craig?'

Craig shook his head, went silent.

Arielle pressed with her question. 'What did the people do?'

Craig snapped his head back up, his eyes pinned so wide open it looked like they were about to burst from his skull. 'They didn't do anything! Nothing, you hear?

They just stood there and let the Dead take them! All of them! Even the bloody kids!'

He fell against Arielle, who held him close like she was trying to squeeze the last of his tears from him.

'I think stopping might be a good idea,' said Lazarus, now seriously worried about Craig. 'You need to check him over, Clair.'

Clair didn't reply. Lazarus reached over to tap her arm and get her attention, but stopped. All the colour had drained from her face and a tear was slipping down her cheek.

'Clair?'

Clair's voice was barely a whisper. And he could see her knuckles go white as she gripped the steering wheel hard; she was terrified. 'What Craig just said ... it's what I saw, when that Dead thing was inside me. When I nearly killed you!'

Lazarus felt like he'd been thrown into a bath of ice.

'You sure?'

Clair nodded slowly, deliberately.

Lazarus turned his head and looked directly at Arielle. 'What's going on? How can Clair remember something Craig just dreamed?'

Arielle said, 'Craig was taken over by one of the Dead, remember?'

'Yes, but not for long,' replied Lazarus. 'I pulled it from him before it took hold.' He hesitated. 'Though, there's something else . . .'

'What?'

'I found him on the other side of the veil with this thing standing over him,' said Lazarus, feeling uncertain. 'It looked like it was drooling something into his mouth.'

'Why didn't you tell me?'

'Didn't seem important,' said Lazarus. 'We killed it, Craig was fine. End of story.'

'Not quite,' said Arielle. 'What Craig just described was no dream. It was a vision of the Dead returning.'

Before Lazarus had a chance to ask what it all meant, Arielle changed the subject completely.

'I want to see if we are being followed. We need to pull over as soon as we can, see what happens. Take the next service station, OK, Clair?'

Clair nodded as a signpost sped into view.

'That's lucky,' said Lazarus. 'There's one just ahead.'

Clair pulled the Defender off the main carriageway. As she steered down the slip road, the Defender shuddered across a few particularly deep potholes filled with oily rain water that shimmered like mercury. The heavy rain made Lazarus feel like they were on a boat in a storm as they lolled left and right.

At the top of the slip road, they saw the service station. The rain looked like it was trying to hammer the place into the ground. People were dashing to and from their cars, hiding under coats and magazines and umbrellas. Clair pulled the Defender into the car park, swung it round and skidded to a halt.

'Now we wait,' said Arielle.

20

BLACK SKY

'So we weren't being followed then,' said Lazarus, his mind still trying to work out what Clair and Craig's dream or vision or whatever it was had meant. He opened the glove compartment and pulled out some biscuits. 'And if that's the case, can we take a walk? We've been in here for hours. I need some fresh air.'

'Not so hasty,' Arielle replied. 'They could have gone past to try and not blow their cover. They could be ahead of us now, just waiting for us to zip past.'

'If someone is following us, why not follow us in here?'

'Because if they are following, they've probably set a trap further ahead,' said Arielle. 'Remember what I said about this being like chess? They're may just be watching us. Someone else will do the dirty work. And walking in here with all these people around; it would be too dangerous. Too obvious.'

Lazarus passed the biscuits to Arielle who gave one to Craig, who took it and nibbled on it disinterestedly. Lazarus was itching to get out now. He wanted to feel the rain on his head and mix among the living, to hear them talking and arguing and rushing around. The thought of it almost excited him.

Arielle opened a locker above Lazarus's head and pulled out two cans, each about the size of a large tin of soup.

'Self-heating meals,' she said, handing them to Lazarus and Craig. 'Taste a bit like military rations, but that's no bad thing. Will certainly fill you up. Clair?'

'Thanks, but I'm not hungry,' said Clair.

Lazarus followed the instructions on the side of his can to work out how to use it. A few minutes later he was chucking the food down his neck. He handed the other back to Arielle who did the same and gave it to Craig.

'I'm still going to take a walk,' Lazarus said.

'Eat first,' said Arielle. 'Then we'll all go. 'Safety in numbers.'

'So are you going to tell us what happened to Craig and Clair or try to pretend it didn't happen?' Lazarus asked.

'I've told you,' said Arielle. 'They were both touched by the Dead. Somehow they saw what the Dead want to do or have planned. That's all I know.'

'I don't believe you,' said Lazarus. He was wolfing down his food at such a rate it was nearly finished. And he was starting to hanker after a decent cheeseburger with fries, onion rings and an illegally-sized Coke.

'Tough,' said Arielle.

Lazarus licked his spoon. 'Right, I'm going to chuck this and go for a stroll. You lot ready?'

He didn't wait for an answer and was out of the door sharpish. He heard Arielle calling after him. He stopped to wait for her, but she was already by his side.

'You move fast.'

'You have no idea,' replied Arielle.

Craig and Clair joined them and together they walked towards the service station, almost as though they were unaware of the rain. Lazarus knew Craig was talking, but his mind was elsewhere. It was like he could hear every conversation around him as people bustled past.

Life was a busy thing and it was here and he was right in it. It felt comforting.

Lazarus headed to the toilets and then slunk around the shop, not really looking at anything. Arielle told him he had five minutes, but she didn't leave him to it. Instead she stood back from the crowds and watched him. If he could have, Lazarus would have tried to escape her. Not for long, but just long enough to be completely on his own in the crowds, away from her ever-reminding stare.

A voice close by.

'Time to get moving again, OK?'

Lazarus looked over to Clair and nodded. He didn't want to leave. He didn't want to get back into that truck and drive off to whatever hellish thing they were about to encounter next. He wanted to stay here and read the ingredients on the sandwich packets, check out the gossip in the magazine racks, stand in the cool breeze humming from the refrigerators of food. Do normal stuff like the normal people around him.

Not a chance.

A few minutes later, he was back in the Defender with

the others, Clair turned the ignition, sparked the engine, and it roared. Steam rose from the bonnet as rain fizzled against the heat. Then they were on their way again, back down to the motorway.

The rain felt even heavier when they got out on to the road, thanks mainly to the speed everyone was doing, and the spray. Everything slowed down. Trucks roared past like super tankers out at sea. Sports cars flew past like speedboats. The world was being washed away, or that's how it looked to Lazarus. And he couldn't help but find himself thinking about how his own life was being washed away too. But rather than torrents of water, it was torrents of blood, and the smell still stuck in his nose, his throat.

Lazarus was pulled from his dark thoughts by a noise from the back.

'Over there,' said Craig, looking behind them, 'it's that car again, isn't it? The one that Clair spotted following us?'

Everyone looked. Clair checked her driver's mirror. Nodded.

'You sure?' asked Lazarus.

'Totally,' said Craig. 'I memorised the number plate.'

Lazarus was impressed. But he was also filled with a sense of dread. That someone had been tailing them for so long told him that more people knew of them than he would have liked to have believed. It didn't matter now where they were heading – they had to lose the black car, and quickly.

'That map,' said Lazarus, pointing to the one Arielle had shown them, 'the one in the net on the roof. Throw it this way – quick!'

Arielle did as she was told. Lazarus liked the sensation of power, but did his best not to show it. He shuffled through the pages, clocked a junction number at the side of the road, and found where they were on the map. It was time to take them off the main road and lose whoever it was that was so interested in where they were heading.

'Take the next exit,' he ordered. 'At the top, hang a left, drive through a junction, take a right, then floor it.'

'Just like that?' said Clair.

'Yeah,' nodded Lazarus. 'Just like that.'

An exit appeared within a few miles. Clair followed

Lazarus's instructions to the letter and soon she'd gone through the traffic lights, hung a right, and now she'd floored it.

'What engine's in this thing?' asked Craig from the back of the Defender. Lazarus turned to see him holding on for his life, but he was smiling, too.

'A very big one,' said Arielle with a faint smile. 'I dumped the original unit and got it replaced. Just didn't have the power I was looking for.'

'I can still see them,' said Clair, glancing into her wing mirror. 'A few cars down, but it's definitely them again. Who are they?'

'And why's it getting so dark?' asked Craig. 'It wasn't bad a few moments ago, and now look at it. It's like a storm's chasing us or something!'

Lazarus looked in the wing mirror. It did look like a storm was gathering, but there was something strange about it. It wasn't like grey clouds of rain were sweeping in. No, this looked like the clouds were being taken over by an oil slick spreading through them, slipping greasily across the sky.

'I've got a bad feeling about this,' said Craig.

The light was fading faster and Lazarus could see the blackness from the sky leaking to the ground beneath, sweeping across it in waves. What the hell was it? Was he making it up?

'Arielle!' he yelled, and jabbed a finger at what he could see. 'You see that too?'

'Yes,' said Arielle.

'What is it?'

'Let's not wait around to find out,' Arielle replied. 'Clair – move!'

Lazarus was studying the map again, trying to ignore the spreading darkness that was getting closer and closer, was almost up with the car behind them now, like it was being dragged along by it. 'Take the next left, then an immediate right,' he commanded without looking up. 'It leads through a woodland, then out on to open moor. It's a straight road for a few miles. Might be able to put some distance between us and then lose them.'

'Agreed,' said Arielle, and almost immediately was swung to her right as Clair pulled the Defender through Lazarus's next set of directions. They were soon in the woodland, but the comfort of its leafy roof was short-lived as they were thrust out the other side and on to the open moors.

'Floor it!' said Arielle.

'But it's too dangerous,' said Clair in terror. 'The road's really bumpy and there are hidden dips all over the place!'

As if it had heard Clair speak, a dip came upon them fast. Lazarus felt his stomach flip as the road dropped out from underneath the vehicle. Too late they all saw the person standing in the middle of the road. Far, far too late to do anything about it.

Everything moved in slow motion.

Clair pushed her whole body into the brake pedal to avoid the collision. The Defender skidded and slid like a tank on ice, started to edge sideways. No one screamed – there wasn't time. When the vehicle eventually came to a stop, it was facing across the road.

Silence.

'Everyone OK?' Lazarus checked.

Out the corner of his eye, he saw the car that had been following them crest the summit of the dip and pile down towards them. The darkness was now thick as velvet, blotting out the world behind them. He threw himself sideways, but was trapped by his seatbelt. The car crunched into the back corner of the Defender, spinning it round even further.

'Gun it!' yelled Arielle at Clair. 'Get us out of here! Now!'

But Clair wasn't given a chance as the driver door was ripped open. Lazarus watched, helpless, as she was sucked out of her seat, the seatbelt snapping in two, then tossed away from the Defender and off the road like she weighed nothing. He saw her land. Heard the dull thud as she impacted. And filling the space where she had been was something he recognised: a creature like the one he'd found stooping over Craig when he'd landed on the other side of the veil in the land of the Dead. But how the hell did it get *here*?

'Arielle!' he yelled as the thing in front of him gripped both sides of the open door with its grey, bony hands, then snapped its mouth with such force Lazarus flinched, half expecting its jaw to fly off. But it just kept on opening, wider and wider. Bones shattered, teeth rained out, but the mouth didn't stop. The wider it got, the more the creature's body shook, like the force of it was close to tearing it apart, limb from limb. And it just kept going, growing larger and larger, taking with it the rest of the creature's face and head until all that remained was a vast mouth sucking Lazarus forward. And in its very centre, tied and twisted in with broken flesh and bone like ribbons, was a swirl of darkness.

Lazarus could feel wind sucking at him. He braced himself against it, but didn't know how long he could hold on. Bits and pieces from inside the vehicle started to fly into the spinning mouth. He watched the empty can from his meal lift out of the foot well and shoot in, only to be torn apart seconds later.

'Arielle!' he shouted again, and just caught sight of her slipping out the back of the Defender. What was she doing – bolting? The creature howled. Lazarus snapped his head back to see it straining as something pulled it back. It howled again, gripped harder. Whatever was pulling it yanked with such force that its hands didn't so much let go, as come off.

'You get Clair,' Arielle commanded, appearing in the doorway and pulling away the bloody hands that still gripped the Defender. Then she was in, door slammed behind. 'I'll drive. Now run!'

Lazarus was out of his door in a breath. He charged round the front of the Defender as Arielle snapped it into life again. Clair was only a few metres away. She was stirring, but couldn't stand. Lazarus skidded on the grass as he came up to her. Then, as he made to lift her, everything slowed and, for the first time, he saw the Dark up close as it rained down from the sky behind the car that had rammed them.

He backed away as it crept towards them, wilting the life from everything it touched, turning the grass black, the flowers to slick lines of rot. Lazarus reached for his spike and held it out like a firebrand, hoping against hope that it would somehow protect them.

The Dark stopped. If it moved closer Lazarus knew it would cut them off from the Defender completely. He pulled Clair up, kept the spike pointed in threat, and started to move. The Dark moved with him. The thing was a bubbling, spitting obsidian blackness. It slipped across the ground like a fat slug. Then it shuddered, its oily surface split horribly, and thick bloody liquid spewed out and splashed on the floor. Something pushed out through the gaping wound; a slime-covered head frozen in an endless scream ...

Lazarus recognised that awful face. and wanted the ground to swallow him up. Whatever he was up against, it was too much. He didn't stand a chance.

'Lazarus?'

Now Clair was trying to pull him along, not the other way around as he'd intended. The Defender was only a few steps away. Lazarus was still staring at the Dark. Why wasn't it attacking them? Why was it staying at a distance?

'Snap out of it, Laz!'

Clair yanked him so hard that he toppled forward and nearly sent them both to the ground. The momentum got them closer to the Defender. Arielle jumped out and was with them in a second.

'Hold on to me!' she said, hitching Clair's arm round her neck. 'In the back, OK? Lazarus – passenger side – now!'

Clair nodded as Lazarus, still dazed by what he'd just seen, ran round the front of the Defender. He was about to jump in when something snapped him round by his shoulder. He didn't give himself a chance to think about what it was and used the momentum to pull the spike from his belt and drive it into the creature. It squealed, tore at the spike with its bloody handless arms, but Lazarus simply shoved it in harder, twisted it, then wrenched it out, booting the creature away from him before throwing himself into the Defender and slamming the door. As he did so, he caught sight in the reflection in the wing mirror of a figure in the rear of the vehicle that had rammed them.

Arielle slammed the back door, Clair now inside. The figure in the vehicle behind them opened theirs and started to climb out.

'Move it, Arielle!' Lazarus yelled.

A moment later Lazarus felt himself pushed back against his seat as Arielle jumped in and slammed the pedal to the floor.

Lazarus chanced a final look in the wing mirror. He could see now that the figure staring at the disappearing Defender was clearly a woman. Like the figure who had taken his father back in the land of the Dead, she had long, grey, matted hair and was dressed all in white. She turned to walk back to her car, and as she did so, Lazarus saw the Dark twist and swirl around her like it was being sucked down a drain. And when it was finally gone, in its place stood a man.

21

☠ ALREADY DEAD ☠

'You OK?'

Lazarus was out of breath, couldn't answer, just mouthed 'Yes' at Arielle as the Defender seemed to pull the world ahead under its wheels and spit it out the back as nothing but muck and grit.

'What got into you back there? And what was that thing?'

Lazarus found his voice. 'I think it was the Dark. But don't quote me on that. Whatever it was, there was someone trapped inside it.'

He didn't want to say who he thought it was. It was too horrible to think about. So he was relieved no one pushed for more information. He turned the conversation towards his best friend.

'Craig?'

'Fine,' said Craig. 'Got off lightly that time. Nothing tried to eat me or rip me apart. Makes a change.'

'What was that?' he asked between gulps of air. 'The same kind of thing attacked us on the other side of the veil. And what's with the swirling, whirlpool thing that sucks you in like it's trying to eat you? I thought dead was dead – what *are* those things?'

'Best way to think of it,' said Arielle, dropping a couple of gears to bounce the Defender round a corner, 'is to not think at all. Hell and the land of the Dead are strange places, Lazarus. Things grow there. Evolve. Whatever it was isn't important. You just need to focus on the fact that the Dead are already slipping through. Which means . . .'

'Dad,' said Lazarus, and his mind was back on the Dark that had come after them just a few minutes ago. Had he really seen his father trapped in that blackness?

Arielle nodded. 'They're already using him to open the veil and send the Dead after you. You're their last threat, Lazarus. They need you out of the way before they do whatever it is they're planning to do. They obviously don't want you turning up and ruining their big plan, whatever that is. Clair and Craig's visions have something to do with it. I just don't know what.'

'But I thought the Dead needed a human body to exist here at all, you know, in the land of the living?' said Lazarus, confused.

'They do,' said Arielle. 'What you saw could happen to any one of you.'

'You mean . . .'

Arielle nodded. 'Whatever that was, it was once a human. And by once, I mean a few hours ago, before it was taken over by one of the Dead.'

Lazarus was shocked. 'But you tore its hands off!'

'And I'd do it again to keep you safe!' Arielle snapped.

'I could've handled it,' said Lazarus, angry as hell. 'I've pulled the Dead out of Clair and Craig, remember?'

For a moment, he experienced both moments again, the horrors of each boiling his blood. He was back in the hospital ward, watching as, with nothing more than his bare hands, he ripped the thing out of Clair. It had been horrific, but Clair had survived. The Dead had squealed as he'd pinned it to the floor with the spike Clair had found – the spike that now rested in his belt. And then with Craig . . . but the pain of that memory, of seeing his best friend taken over by one of the Dead, was too much and he pushed it away again.

'The correct term is eviction,' said Arielle, her voice quiet, almost in pain. 'And yes, I do remember.'

'I could've saved them!' Lazarus yelled. 'You never even gave me a chance!'

'Whoever it was,' said Arielle, and Lazarus could see tears in her eyes, 'what the thing inside them did, there was no surviving it. They were already dead, Lazarus. Already dead.'

Lazarus slumped back in his seat and closed his eyes. He'd assumed the creature had been like the one he'd seen before, but he'd been wrong. He saw flashbacks of it playing in the darkness of his mind, the way it had twisted its head into that screaming vortex of violence that had tried to suck him in. It was no way for anyone to die. No way at all. He felt a flicker of rage turn to a flame way down inside. Even more so when he thought of his dad trapped in the Dark. What pain was he in, he wondered? What kind of torture was he suffering? And was there any way to rescue him, bring him home?

He opened his eyes, tried to ignore the questions racing

through his head. 'Who was the other person in the car?'

'What other person?' asked Craig and Lazarus looked round to see his friend checking Clair was OK.

'There was a woman in the car,' Clair was holding her head in her hands. 'I saw her, too. All in white.'

Craig's eyes flicked up to catch Lazarus's. 'The same people who threw the brick wrapped in your picture at us before we set off, right? Those pawns Arielle was on about.'

'Probably been following us all the way,' said Arielle. 'An opportunity presented itself and they took it. They're getting brave, daring. Not a good sign.'

'Whoever it was,' said Lazarus, 'we need to get to Abaddon now. We need to stop it, before it gets any worse. Before the Dead take any more victims.'

'I just hope he's taking visitors,' said Arielle. 'Like I said, it's been a long, long time . . .'

The rest of the journey continued without hitch or event. If anything, it was dull. It didn't stop raining. The sky refused to brighten. Lazarus tried to doze off, resting his head against the cold window. But he kept waking up.

He'd seen too much and his mind refused to rest. There were too many questions to deal with and not enough answers. And the more he searched – the deeper he got into this world of being the Keeper – the further away he seemed to be from coming out of it with his dad at his side.

In the twilight moments between restless sleep, he'd glanced around at the others. Arielle was looking better with every passing moment, her body healing quicker than was medically possible. That made him think about what she'd said about his own ability to recover. What had he taken from her and Red that had so affected him? Was he no longer quite human? What was it Red had said about having death in him? Always with the riddles. And then there was the second spike he'd found in the Defender. An angelic weapon. And he had one of his own. He had no real idea of the power that it held. The idea frightened and excited him. His mind turned to Craig and Clair. Lazarus thought about Craig's headaches, that shared dream or vision that Clair had experienced too.

Lazarus closed his eyes again and shook his head. There was so much going on in there it felt like it would start leaking out of his ears. When he opened his eyes again, Arielle was indicating left.

'How long till we get to the Brock Stone and Abaddon?' Lazarus asked.

'Just over an hour I would think,' said Arielle. 'Try to get a little more rest. You're going to need it.'

Lazarus said no more and turned to look out of the window. Craig and Clair were both fast asleep in the back. A break in the clouds showed, and briefly a stab of sunlight cut through the world outside. Lazarus watched it chase across the fields, slicing through walls and trees and barns like it wanted to make the most of its briefest of moments in the world. Then it was gone, crushed to nothing by clouds pushing against each other. And soon Lazarus felt his eyes grow heavy, and he just went with it.

'We're nearly there. Ten minutes max.'

Lazarus snapped his eyes open to find the Defender threading itself down a narrow lane lined with ancient dry-stone walls. And Arielle wasn't exactly holding back on the throttle.

'What if someone comes round one of these bends?'

asked Lazarus, pushing himself back in his seat to be as far away from the front of the vehicle as possible.

'Then they'd better get out of the way,' said Arielle.

Lazarus heard Craig pull himself up off the floor. 'How long have I been out?'

'Dunno,' said Lazarus. 'I've only just woken up myself.'

'The Brock Stone is just over there,' said Arielle, pointing with her left hand as she swung the Defender round a sharp hairpin and on to a section of the road cutting across open moor. Though it didn't make it any safer. At each side, the ground dipped and rose in a succession of heather-topped mounds, leading off into towering slopes.

'Tractor!' screamed Clair.

Lazarus saw it. They all did. It filled the road ahead.

'Hold on!' shouted Arielle.

Dropping a gear and with a yank of the steering wheel, she threw the Defender off the road and on to the moor. For a split second Lazarus felt himself rise off his seat as the vehicle grabbed air. Then it bounced down and chewed its way ahead, the back end sliding round.

Arielle caught it, pulled it back, accelerated, bounced them back on to the road.

'Fun this, isn't it?' said Arielle. 'Now you know why I drive this and not a nice little family saloon.'

'Yeah, because you're mental,' said Craig.

Arielle didn't let up. The moment with the tractor had obviously passed Arielle by as a learning experience. Lazarus hoped the journey would end soon. And that they'd survive it.

At last, Arielle pulled the Defender into a large parking area. It went in sideways, sending out a wave of gravel large enough to surf, then stopped.

'Out.'

Lazarus yanked open the door and fell out into what was left of the day. The rain had eased but it was getting darker: not just because the day was drawing on, but because the clouds above looked like they were getting thicker. The mountains around them slowly slipped behind the cloud, disappearing silently from sight, almost as though they were trying to hide.

'That's the Brock Stone,' said Arielle, pointing into a field at a vast, lonely boulder as she walked round to the back of the Defender to open the door for Clair and Craig.

'It's huge,' said Lazarus. The thing was as big as a bus. Two buses even.

'Left here by the glacier that carved out this little valley,' said Arielle. 'I tell you, that was something to see.'

Lazarus blinked. 'You saw the *glacier*?'

Arielle didn't reply – she was in the back of the Defender and Craig and Clair were now outside.

'Jeez,' said Craig. 'That thing looks like the rest of the world's afraid of it. I mean, it just looks so angry.'

The sound of the Defender door clanging shut rattled around the hills.

'Come on, then,' said Arielle, handing out torches. 'let's go wake Abaddon.'

'Do I want to know why we need these?' asked Craig.

'Not yet.'

Arielle headed towards the stone.

'We'll find out all too soon,' said Lazarus. 'Come on – she really shifts when she wants to.'

Lazarus jogged ahead, leading the way, and soon they caught up with Arielle. The air smelled rich and green, thanks to all the rain. The occasional bleat of a sheep or two rang out, though Lazarus hadn't a clue where from. This was a big and empty place. Getting lost would be all too easy.

When they reached the stone, it was even bigger than they'd imagined. It rose out of the ground like the only way it could ever have ended up there was to have grown like a vast, rock mushroom. Lazarus hesitated to get too close. In the silence of the valley, and as the rain started again, it felt to him as though the stone knew they were there and that they wanted something. He was pretty sure it wasn't too happy about it.

'Now what?' asked Craig.

Without a word, Arielle launched herself skyward. Lazarus had never seen anything like it. The Brock Stone must have been at least fifteen feet high, but she simply jumped from a standing start and landed gently on the top.

'That was pretty impressive,' said Craig. 'No wires or anything.'

But Lazarus wasn't listening. He was staring at Arielle now standing on top of the stone. In the grey light and rain, she looked terrible and frightening. Her long coat billowed around her, slapping at her legs, and her hair danced above her head like it was trying to pull the cloud down around her. She slipped her sword from its scabbard, adding to the spectacle. Then she raised it above her head and drove the blade down in a sharp arc to clank against the stone at her feet.

His ears ringing from the sound, Lazarus was amazed to see that the sword was still in one piece. With the force Arielle had used, it should have snapped in half. But no, it was undamaged, and she slipped it back into its scabbard before leaping silently back down to join them, the flapping tails of her coat the only noise.

'What did you just do?' asked Lazarus, racing after Arielle as she walked away from the stone and further into the valley.

'I just knocked on Abaddon's front door,' she said. She pulled a wine bottle out from the inside of her coat, biting out the cork and spitting it away. 'And now I'm going to let myself in.'

'Front door?' said Clair. 'That was a stone! Where are we going?'

They rounded a large mound of tufty ground and found themselves in a small, crescent-shaped area that was sheltered from the rain and wind a little. A small stream ran down the middle. And it was where it was flowing from that soon grabbed their attention.

'You're not serious,' said Clair.

'I'm afraid so,' said Arielle, and drank deep from the bottle. A drop slipped red and quiet from the corner of her mouth and down her chin to fall on to her jacket.

It was a small, rotten wooden door, flecked with blue paint, sitting almost sadly under an arch of old stone and set into the side of the hill rising above them. It couldn't have been much more than a metre high.

'Looks like the kind of door a troll would live behind,' said Craig. 'Or some Stephen King creation.'

Lazarus stared at the door. 'This is where the torches come in, right?'

Arielle smiled. 'I hope none of you are claustrophobic.'

22

☠☠ SLIMY DARKNESS ☠☠

'Ladies first,' said Craig and stood back to allow Clair past.

'I hope you're not suggesting I'm no lady,' said Arielle. Craig spluttered. Arielle laughed.

It was a strange sound, thought Lazarus, considering what they were doing and the place they were in. It didn't seem to fit right. The sound fluttered around like a bird trapped in a cage before finally dying away. But he was struck by its clarity, like it was the blueprint of all laughter, an example of how it should sound but rarely did. It was almost musical.

'Just follow me,' said Arielle walking over to the door and crouching down, just to one side of the flowing water. She lifted the wine bottle again, then rested it to its side, empty. 'You'll need those torches. I've spare batteries if they start to die on us. Keep your heads low and try not to think of the millions of tons of rock above you just waiting to come crashing down.'

'You're rubbish at motivational speeches,' said Craig.

'Wasn't in the job description,' Arielle replied.

'And drinking wine like water was?' said Clair.

Arielle wiped her mouth and leant across to the metal clasp holding the door shut, kneeling in the water as she did so. With a heave, she pulled the door open. It complained at first, then eventually gave up and swung open on hinges rusted deep into the stone arch that surrounded it. She flicked on her own torch and jabbed it at the darkness. It didn't have much effect, almost as though the dark was pushing the light away.

Lazarus stared and was soon able to make out rusted rails set into the floor of the tunnel. 'What is this place?' he asked.

'It's an old mine,' said Arielle. 'Closed a long, long time ago. The network of tunnels under here is extraordinary, especially when you think they were dug out by pickaxe and a little bit of blasting dynamite.'

'Sounds dangerous,' said Clair.

'It is,' replied Arielle edging through the arch and into the slimy darkness on the other side. 'Go where I go, and don't stray. You get lost down here, not even God would be able to find you.'

'Always with the happy thoughts,' said Craig.

'Right, let's get this over and done with,' said Lazarus. Pushing his own fear of what they were doing way down into his belly, he edged in through the arch after Arielle. Clair and Craig followed.

Lazarus kept his head as low as possible. The floor was strewn with rock and gravel, and water was running freely over it, freezing his skin, drenching him. Soon he couldn't feel anything in his knees and feet, not even when they crunched on a large stone. Now and again he'd look up just to check on Arielle, and behind to Clair and Craig, but all that did was make him even more aware of the size of the tunnel they were navigating. They were already so deep that no light from outside could reach them. If their torches gave out Lazarus knew he wouldn't be able to see his hand in front of his face, not even if it was touching his nose.

Lazarus lost track of time as they crawled. It seemed

endless and time lost all meaning. The air was cool and smelt strange. It reminded Lazarus of how beer smelt when you popped the lid off a bottle fresh from the fridge. Not that he drank beer that much. But sometimes Craig would turn up with a couple of bottles and they'd chill them for a couple of hours before sinking them to a movie. But that kind of thing seemed a long time ago now. Would he ever experience it again?

Ahead, Arielle stopped.

'What's up?' asked Lazarus.

'Nothing,' said Arielle. 'Soon we'll be able to walk. The roof of the tunnel rises. But from then on we need to keep an eye out for deads.'

'Are you taking the piss? Because it's not funny.'

'I didn't say *the Dead*,' replied Arielle. 'Deads are false floors made of wooden planks. Miners used them when tunnels crossed over each other. Some have tons of rocks piled on top of them.'

'Nice safety tip,' said Craig, as he and Clair came to a halt behind Lazarus.

'Always looking out for you,' said Arielle. She continued forward, leading them further into the mountainside.

Just like she'd said, the tunnel was soon high enough for them to walk in, but no less claustrophobic. Lazarus had never had a problem with small spaces. But being down here now, he realised he'd never really experienced them. The occasional lift or crowded room had nothing on being stuck down a mine under millions of tons of rock, in a tunnel that you could only walk through in single file.

Further down the tunnel, Lazarus noticed the occasional dark and eerie opening in the tunnel walls. Some were head height, others needed crawling into. None of them looked inviting. And the air that sat just at the entrances was old and stale, and stuck in the back of Lazarus's throat. He figured he'd be sticking to Arielle's advice and not exploring any of them. Being stuck down here was a petrifying thought. There would be no way out, just the last moments of life spent wandering blindly from passage to passage till a fall finished you off or you froze or starved to death. Nice.

Eventually the tunnel widened. Craig got excited when they found an old miner's cart still on the rails where it had been abandoned God knew how many years ago.

It was filled with rubble and by one of its wheels, Clair found an old oil lamp lying on its side. It wasn't exactly in working order, but it was a haunting reminder of the numerous lives that had worked the mine and were now nothing but memories that only the mountain could recall. It was a cold and creepy place, and Lazarus was looking forward to getting back outside and tasting fresh air again.

'We're coming to the end of the tunnel,' said Arielle, falling back to walk alongside Lazarus.

'It's just ahead – look,' and she shone her torch ahead. It sent a conical yellow beam into the nothingness beyond and Lazarus was just about able to make out a cavern. As they walked in, the ceiling rose to about forty feet and the sound of dripping water echoed with an almost metallic ring. But it wasn't the cavern that drew Lazarus's attention. It was the black pool of water that filled half of it and seemed to slip silent and still beneath the far wall.

'I don't like the look of that,' said Craig, edging forward. 'How deep is it?'

Lazarus picked up a stone and lobbed it. It cast a silent

arc through the darkness, cut through his torch beam, then broke the mirror-still surface of the pool with a deep, dull plop.

'Deep,' said Lazarus, then realised something. 'If this is the end of the tunnel, then why are we here? I thought we came to find Abaddon, but there's nothing here. Arielle, what's . . .'

But what he saw silenced him immediately.

Arielle was slipping out of her boots, her jacket and sword already off. Next she unbelted the revolver Lazarus had last seen when she'd pulled it on him and shot him straight through the heart.

'She's not thinking of doing what I think she's thinking of doing . . . is she?' asked Craig.

'Yeah, I think she is,' said Lazarus, but he wasn't given a chance to stop her.

Without warning, Arielle switched off her torch and dived in. And as she slipped through the surface of the water, she hardly made a sound or a splash.

Lazarus ran to the edge of the pool, Craig and Clair close behind.

'That water's freezing!' said Clair in horror. 'If she

doesn't die of the shock, she'll have hypothermia in minutes. What was she thinking?'

'I don't reckon she thinks at all,' said Craig. 'Kind of acts more on impulse. Maybe it's an angel thing. You know, we all think that angels are these weird beings dressed in white with huge wings and haloes, when in fact they're all adrenaline freaks and danger junkies.'

'That's it,' said Clair. 'I'm not listening to another word you say. Ever.'

'Shush!' hushed Lazarus, staring into the pool. 'I think she's coming back.'

Almost in slow motion, Arielle's head raised itself out of the water. The rest of her followed as she pulled herself gracefully out of the pool. She was drenched, but didn't seem at all concerned. And when she spoke, her voice was steady and calm, rather than chattering with the cold.

'Take this,' she said, handing the end of a rope to Lazarus. The other end was somewhere under the water. 'Tie it round that rock over there, OK?'

Lazarus did as he was told. 'I don't really want to know the answer to this,' he said, 'but what's the rope for?'

Arielle leant down and picked it up. 'It's only a short swim,' she said, water dripping from the rope, through her slim fingers and to the floor. 'Just follow this and you'll be through in seconds.'

Lazarus, Craig and Clair were speechless.

Arielle grinned. 'Who's going first?'

23
☠☠☠ SLAUGHTERED FAMILY ☠☠☠

Lazarus stared at the pool, the tips of his shoes almost touching the surface. The water was so black it looked solid, like he could just walk out on it. But it was also drawing him in, daring him to take a dip so it could swallow him up forever, have him drifting under the mountains on the currents of hidden streams for centuries until his body finally dissolved to nothing.

'Why is it,' he asked, 'that no matter what we do or where we go, there's always something worse round the next corner?'

'Doesn't make me want to find out what's on the other side of this pool,' said Craig.

'It's easy,' said Arielle. 'The pool is a sump, which is basically a part of a cave where the roof meets water and the only way through is to take a very deep breath.'

Lazarus was still staring at the water. 'How deep?'

'About five metres,' said Arielle. 'It's over in seconds. Just grab the rope and pull yourself along. The roof dips a bit so you go down before you go up.'

Lazarus still wasn't convinced. Why hadn't Arielle told them this was at the end of the mine tunnel? Mind you, he thought, if she had, he wouldn't have even made it this far.

'I'm not sure what's worse,' said Craig, 'being chased by the Dead, or jumping into that.'

'Look, if we're going to find Abaddon, then we have to go through,' said Arielle. 'It's as simple as that.'

'You said no one had seen him for *centuries*,' said Lazarus. 'So how come that rope's there?'

'Because I put it there,' said Arielle. 'A very long time ago. Now please, can we get a move on?'

Lazarus tried to stop himself backing away, but couldn't. Just the thought of his head dropping beneath the surface, then under rock ... It sent shivers through him that threatened to split his skin right open.

'You're really not into this, are you?' asked Craig.

Lazarus shook his head.

'What's wrong? It's just a pool of water, isn't it? A cold one, but just water.'

But to Lazarus it was more than that, so much more. It wasn't just water. It was a trap. A thing that dragged you down, sucked the breath from your lungs then filled them with liquid, and watched as you choked and coughed and panicked your way to a terrifying death.

'I'm amazed,' said Craig. 'You've seen and done stuff this last few days that'd have most people running scared for the rest of their lives! Come on Laz, it'll be fine!'

Lazarus wanted to be brave. He wanted to be able to just run to that pool, leap in and go for it. But he couldn't. Not a chance.

'OK,' said Craig, 'I'll tell you what. I'll go first. If I can do it, then you can, right?'

Lazarus nodded weakly, but a splash from behind them made them both turn round. A circle of bubbles and ripples was spreading out on the pool's surface.

'Clair . . .'

'No way,' said Craig. 'Seriously?'

'Totally,' said Lazarus. 'Her shoes are over by Arielle's. And Arielle's over there staring at us like we're a pair of total losers.'

Craig glanced over at Arielle. 'Well we can't have that, can we?' He bent over, pulled off his shoes, jogged to Arielle and handed them over. Then he turned and dived head first into the wet darkness.

Now, thought Lazarus, it's just me.

Arielle waved him over. He strolled as slowly as he could, one eye on the pool at all times, like he was half expecting some big, water-dwelling monster to burst out and rip his rib cage with a single flick of a tentacle.

'I was going to keep you until last anyway,' said Arielle. 'I need to tell you something.'

'That I don't have to go through?'

Arielle said, 'Sadly, no. You have to go through. It's about Abaddon.'

Lazarus didn't like late warnings. Particularly when they were about people who were dead and who he was about to meet. 'What's wrong?'

'Look,' said Arielle, 'the only reason for Red to send us to Abaddon is that things really are about to get very bad indeed.'

'If you're trying to reassure me . . .' said Lazarus.

Arielle's stare was unwavering and drove through Lazarus like ice. 'I'm doing anything but,' she said. 'Whether he knows anything about this Dark stuff you and Craig spoke about, I don't know. But I do know that when it comes to the Dead, no one – and I do mean *no one* – is ever allowed to stand in his way.'

Lazarus was very aware of being alone in the dark with Arielle. 'Why are only telling me this?' he demanded. 'What about the other two?'

'Because,' said Arielle, 'Abaddon will only be interested in you. They're safe. You're not.'

'I don't understand,' said Lazarus, getting more than a little tired of always feeling so confused or going into a situation without enough information on what to expect, or how to deal with it if it tried to kill him.

'With Abaddon,' said Arielle, 'this is personal. It's not just about stopping the Dead coming back, it's about eradicating them for good. And as far as he's concerned, you – and I – are as much a part of the problem as the solution. Though I'm hoping time has mellowed him a little.'

'And we're here to ask for his help?'

Arielle nodded. 'It seems so, yes. And I'm afraid he is not blessed with a forgiving nature. Or compassion. Or mercy.'

'From what I've seen of the Dead,' said Lazarus, 'that seems to make sense.'

'You're forgetting,' said Arielle, 'that the Dead can still redeem themselves. There's still that slim hope that some will move on. Though most don't.'

'That sounds way too metaphysical,' said Lazarus.

'I know,' said Arielle. 'It even makes my head hurt, and I've been around for a long, long time.'

Lazarus was very conscious of the fact that Craig and Clair were now either drowned or on the other side of the sump. If he was going to do this, he wanted to get it over and done with, not stand around chatting. But he needed to know more about Abaddon.

'Why is it personal then?' he asked. 'What happened?'

Arielle sat down on a large, flat rock. She picked up a stone and spun it across the surface of the pool. 'Around four hundred years ago,' she said, reaching for another stone, 'he was a priest. A good one, too. Very much the shepherd looking after his flock. Then one day, when he went to lock up his church . . .'

Arielle's head tipped forward, covering her face with her black, bedraggled hair. She sat up again, pushing it back over her head.

'There was this gang of thieves,' Arielle continued, and Lazarus could tell what she was saying was upsetting her terribly. 'They were in the church, ripping it apart for gold. Stealing anything they could move. And if it didn't move, they ripped it off. Even took the money that was collected for the poor. When they saw Abaddon, they grabbed him and decided to teach him a lesson for being such a good little priest.'

'What?' asked Lazarus, itching to hear the end of the story. 'What did they do?'

Arielle swallowed hard. 'They forced him to watch as they slaughtered his family. Wife, children, every last one of them dead. When they turned on him, he somehow managed to escape, and disappeared into the night.'

Lazarus felt cold. Was this true? It had to be, he guessed, but it sounded so violent, so wrong.

'What happened then?' asked Lazarus. 'I can't see why he'd be thrown out of the church.'

'He could no longer be a priest after what he did next,' said Arielle. 'You see, he was in the business of forgiveness. He knew the sales pitch better than anyone. And he knew revenge was both terrible and addictive.'

'Addictive?'

'Oh yeah,' said Arielle. 'You see, Abaddon hadn't always been a priest. He had a pretty black past. He'd been a soldier who survived a fair number of battlefields; a sharpshooter, and more than a little handy with a sword too. After that he spent a few months roaming the streets, brawling and drinking and getting into trouble. After that he took up with some poachers. Got pretty good too, what with his army background. And then . . .'

Another pause. Lazarus wanted Arielle just to get to the end of it.

'And then what?'

Arielle raised her head and their eyes met. 'He met me,' she said. Her voice was suddenly feather soft, like it could just float away. 'It changed everything for him. More completely than I could've expected. The man was a killer, Lazarus! I mean, he'd done things too horrific to describe. And then he became a priest! I was blinded by the goodness I saw in him under all that muck and grime. But then, I could never have foreseen what would happen to his family. Or what happened after.'

'What did he do?'

Lazarus had a terrible feeling about what he was about to hear. But he still wanted to hear it, no matter how bad it was.

'He tracked down the leader of the gang,' said Arielle. 'Found him shacked up in an old inn. Still in his priest's garb, he walked over to the leader at the bar and just tapped him on the shoulder. When the man turned, he found himself staring down the wrong end of a flintlock pistol. By good fortune or luck, it misfired. But the flame scorched the man's face and destroyed one eye. Abaddon was dragged away.'

'Did he go to prison?'

'No,' said Arielle. 'Even though everyone knew what had happened to Abaddon's family, the story was hushed up. The gang leader had a reputation, and no one dared do anything because rumours about him were rife. He dabbled in things best left well alone. Dark things.'

Lazarus caught on straight away. 'The gang's leader

was working for the Dead, wasn't he?'

'Yes,' said Arielle, 'just that. And he wasn't only into stealing gold – that he did for profit and a bit of fun. He was also stealing people for the Dead to possess and take over. He was a bad man, Lazarus – a very bad man. And his gang was worse if anything.'

'And that's why Abaddon was thrown out of the church – for what he did to the gang leader?'

'Totally,' said Arielle. 'They couldn't have a priest preaching love and forgiveness on Sunday, then spending the rest of the week on bloody revenge. So Abaddon was defrocked. He disappeared almost immediately. No one thought anything of it; they just felt sorry for him. But then a few months later, the gang started to turn up dead, all found hanging from trees surrounding the church that had once been Abaddon's. And each one had a mirror strapped in front of their face so they could watch their own death. A dark twist of Abaddon's as they'd forced him to watch the death of his own family, which had essentially killed him.'

Lazarus was beginning to wonder if he wanted to meet Abaddon at all.

'But what happened?' He felt almost breathless with what Arielle was telling him. 'You said he's dead, but he's not *one* of the Dead. So what is he? How can he still be around?'

'Abaddon had no idea about the Dead or how they operated. This wasn't the only gang. There were others. And they were called in. They stirred up Abaddon's parish with false tales and stories that painted him as a devil. They turned on him, helped track him down, then strung him up from the tower of his own church. Murdered by the very people he had cared for.'

'Ouch,' said Lazarus.

Arielle raised a finger to point it at Lazarus. 'Except Abaddon refused to die. When he found out what had gone on behind the scenes, rage consumed him utterly. He wanted to fight the Dead and stop them returning by any means, fair or foul. He made a deal with Red. No one knows how it happened, or why, but Red agreed and Abaddon came back to continue his, for want of a better word, work. And he did it with such ferocious violence that we had to rein him in.'

'Red brought him back to life?'

'No,' said Arielle. 'The only way for Abaddon to return was as one of the Dead, but uniquely, in his own body.'

'That's impossible!' said Lazarus. 'Dead bodies don't last long enough, do they? Even I know that and I'm new at this.'

'That depends,' said Arielle. 'Abaddon embalmed himself, removed his internal organs, did the lot. It's pretty damned freaky if you ask me, but that's what he did. And now he lies in a stone sarcophagus filled with fluid that keeps him preserved. But other things aid it: he's just about as close to indestructable as you can get. And he's waiting.'

'What for?'

'At this moment in time,' said Arielle, 'you.'

Lazarus was quiet, trying to take it all in. Then he said, 'So we're back to the pool, aren't we?'

Arielle nodded.

'But I can't,' said Lazarus. 'It's not that I don't want to, it's just that . . .'

His voice faded but he could hear his heartbeat going totally nuts.

'Why are you so afraid?' asked Arielle. 'You can swim, can't you?'

Lazarus was silent.

'Please tell me you can swim, Lazarus,' said Arielle.

'No, I can't,' said Lazarus. 'I'm scared of water.'

'Why didn't you tell me?' asked Arielle, her voice rising. 'Why didn't you let me know?'

'Because,' shouted Lazarus, 'you never asked!'

24

☠☠☠ WAITING MONSTER ☠☠☠

'Look, I nearly drowned at school, when I was seven,' sighed Lazarus. He really didn't want to say any of this out loud. It made him feel weak and pathetic and embarrassed. 'Someone threw me in at the deep end. I was dragged out, resuscitated. Kind of put me off.'

He hated talking about it, not that he could remember much of what happened. He'd been terrified of water ever since – and had never learnt to swim. Considering how old he was, he now felt a total dick about it and kept it quiet. At what point was being scared of water cool?

'You need to stop dying, Laz,' said Arielle. 'It's a killer of a habit.'

'You're not funny.'

'No, you're right, I'm not,' said Arielle, and before Lazarus could react, she grabbed him and dragged him towards the pool. He did his best to drive his heels into the ground, to stop himself. It didn't work. Despite looking like she'd snap if someone near her burped, Arielle was hugely strong. 'I'm not going in!'

'No choice,' said Arielle. 'Now hold your breath!'

Lazarus struggled one last time before he felt his feet leave the ground. Then his world went black and cold.

Under the water, Lazarus kept his eyes open. He was too scared to shut them. Bubbles sped past him. He could see Arielle powering them along with just one arm. And she wasn't using the rope to guide her – he noticed that most of all. What if she went the wrong way? What then? What if they ran out of air? She'd probably be fine, being an angel weirdo. But him? He'd be choking on cave water and coughing his life out in this forgotten hole before she even noticed.

Light flashed ahead. Thin streaks of it reaching down through the water. They were slipping under a sharp crag of rock that would easily cut them in half if it fell. More light. A strange dappling just above. Then they crashed through it. And breathed.

If Lazarus hadn't been dependent on Arielle to get him

to the other side of the pool, he'd have happily chinned her one. 'You mentalist!' he screamed. 'You're insane! I could've drowned!'

Hands grabbed him and pulled.

'Hi Laz,' said Craig. 'What took you so long?'

Lazarus was more than a little bit relieved to see Craig and he allowed himself to be pulled from the water like a bedraggled spaniel. Standing at last on solid ground, he shook with cold, coughed and spat.

'Learn to bloody well swim,' said Arielle, sliding out of the pool. 'Seriously, at your age, there's no excuse. It could save your life. And it seems you need all the help you can get in that area.'

'But you just chucked me in!' shouted Lazarus. 'That's not normal. Particularly not for someone so keen on keeping me alive!'

Arielle ignored him and checked that Clair and Craig were OK.

'You're not shivering,' said Lazarus. 'And you're almost dry. How's that possible?'

Then he noticed something about the cavern he'd come out in. It was warm, strangely so, like the rocks themselves were generating heat.

'Arielle, what's with the heat?'

She said but one word: 'Abaddon.'

Lazarus threw his hands in the air. 'Oh, great, so now he's not just dead and a crazed killer, but he has some freaky flame power?'

'No,' said Arielle. 'He just likes it warm, that's all.'

Lazarus remembered his first meeting with Red, how he'd found him in front of a roaring fire in the front room, loading it with fresh logs. Red had complained of the cold. Lazarus wondered for a moment if all of the Dead found it cold on this side of the veil. But was Red actually dead? Lazarus didn't think so. He decided to stop thinking for a moment – it was making his brain hurt.

Arielle walked across the cavern to a huge pile of rocks Lazarus hadn't noticed when he'd first popped up out of the water. Neither had he noticed the huge candles standing in alcoves all around the cavern, their soft yellow light pushing the darkness back into the pool. He guessed they had a lot to do with the warmth. There were so many of them, and those high in the roof looked like they were floating in a bubble of their own light.

'They're totally Hammer House of Horror, aren't they?' said Craig, seeing that Lazarus had noticed the candles. 'Vincent Price would love it here!'

Lazarus went for a closer look. The candles burned with an odd flame. They didn't flicker or spit and the wax didn't seem to be melting. The science bugged him for a second. With so many candles burning, how much oxygen did they have left in the place before they suffocated? But that thought fluttered away on a faint breeze that caught him from the side. He turned to find the source but couldn't see anything. At least they weren't going to suffocate.

'They were lit when we arrived,' said Craig, knocking Lazarus from his thoughts of impending death. 'I figured Arielle had lit them.'

'No,' said Arielle. 'Just another strangeness of the place. They're always burning.'

'It's a bit creepy,' said Clair. 'And it's a dead end again. If this Abaddon person is here, I can't see where.'

'But I can smell him,' said Lazarus.

He hadn't noticed it at first. He'd been too scared by his near-death experience in the sump. And then there was the church-like smell of the candles burning in the cavern. But now he could taste death in the back of his throat. It wasn't strong enough to make his head spin out, and even if it had been, he'd have been able to cope – he could control the nausea now, thankfully.

'So where is he, then?' asked Craig.

Lazarus tried to follow the smell. It was so faint, almost completely hidden, but he knew it was there, that Abaddon was close. His eyes fell on the pile of rocks and rubble by Arielle. And he pointed.

'There,' he said. 'That's where the smell's coming from.'

Craig and Clair followed Lazarus over to Arielle. Clair pulled a rock loose, watched another one fall into its place. 'He's under here?'

Arielle nodded slowly. 'We . . . I mean, I . . . Well, let's just say that we didn't want him getting out without an invitation first.'

'It's going to take hours to shift that lot,' said Craig.

Arielle's reply wasn't exactly said in jest.

'Then we'd best get started then, hadn't we?'

With little enthusiasm and even less energy, Lazarus,

Craig and Clair set to with the rocks. Arielle, though, worked with an impossible and relentless energy. They couldn't believe how she'd recovered so well from the state she'd been just a few hours ago. They all cut their hands, grazed them, wiped blood on their clothes and kept going. At first it was a thankless job as every stone moved was replaced by another. Finally though, the pile decreased and after an hour of lugging rocks across the cavern, they were able to see what they'd been digging for.

Craig was the first to find it. 'I think I've found a corner.'

With renewed enthusiasm, they pulled away the rocks until Abaddon's resting place was revealed.

Lazarus stepped back. The smell had been getting stronger the closer they got, but now with the thing fully revealed, it was full-on. He ignored the nausea, locking it away in some part of his brain.

'Nice, isn't it?' said Arielle. 'Not exactly the kind of place I'd rest my head, but Abaddon is pretty unique.'

Clair slipped back across the floor, climbing over rocks for a closer look. 'I thought these were just patterns carved into the stone,' she said, leaning into the surface of the sarcophagus. 'But they're not. They're names and dates, all scratched into the stone.'

Clair was right. Hundreds of names sat in silence on the stone. Dead names, Lazarus guessed.

'Abaddon's victims,' said Arielle. 'Each and every one of them.'

Lazarus reached out and touched one of the names. A flash seared through his mind. Images of untold violence. A lynch mob screaming, carrying burning brands. People snarling, trying to escape a black shadow that follows them relentlessly. A man strung up by his neck from a solitary tree. A family, happy and smiling, unaware that behind them a beast is prowling. A man weeping in a graveyard, clawing at the dirt. Red . . .

Lazarus opened his eyes to find himself staring up at Craig, Clair and Arielle. Clair was checking his pulse.

'You passed out when you touched the sarcophagus,' she said. 'Just crumpled on the spot. What happened? How do you feel?'

'I . . . I don't know,' said Lazarus, sitting up. 'I saw images, like flashbacks but they weren't mine. Horrible things.'

He did his best to describe what he'd seen. Arielle looked at the sarcophagus. 'Abaddon,' she said. 'This place is alive with his essence. You caught some of that when you touched that thing he lies in.'

'What were those images?'

'The reasons for Abaddon becoming who he now is,' said Arielle. 'Both what was done to him, and what he did.'

'I saw his family . . .'

'Then you understand what drove him to become the creature we are about to wake.'

Craig cleared his throat. 'Look, I hope you don't mind me butting in, but is there something you're not telling us about this Abaddon bloke? I know he's dead, but I'm sensing he's more than a little bit dangerous.'

Arielle was quiet.

'Tell them,' Lazarus ordered Arielle. 'They need to know what they're facing.'

'It could do them more harm,' said Arielle. 'Sometimes it is best to know nothing of the monster waiting for you in the dark.'

'I beg to differ,' said Clair. 'Lazarus? What

has she told you?'

Lazarus was sure he felt the air thicken at that moment, like it was preparing itself for something.

'Tell them.'

Arielle nodded. And when she had finished speaking, neither Clair nor Craig said a word. But Lazarus could see what they were thinking written on their faces. They looked terrified and trapped. Lazarus felt exactly the same.

'When I open this,' Arielle said, indicating the sarcophagus, 'you must promise to say nothing, not until I have spoken to him. I must make him understand that we have come for his help. If he thinks otherwise . . .'

But she was cut off. Not by another voice, but by the deep rumble of stone sliding on stone, as the lid of the sarcophagus slid sideways and on to the floor and a vinegary smell stung the air.

25

☠ LEATHERY FREAK ☠

'Quiet!' hissed Arielle, her eyes not moving from the darkness inside the sarcophagus. 'Remember what I said – say *nothing* until I have spoken to him, OK? Red sent us to Abaddon for a reason, and that reason is something to do with the Dark, and what the Dead want to do with it. We need him on our side, not going out on some insane one-man crusade again!'

Lazarus's heel splashed into the still water of the pool, and he thought now that this Abaddon was not a good idea. They were waking one devil to kill another. For a second he wondered if his dad would approve. But there was nothing he could do about it now. He had to trust Arielle.

They all did.

Clair gasped.

She was shaking. All colour had slipped from her face and into the shadows. She raised a quivering finger. Lazarus expected to see Abaddon. But he was wrong. Very wrong.

First he thought it was a trick of the candlelight; the names carved into the side of the sarcophagus looked different. But it was no trick. The words were weeping flame to the floor, thin rivulets of molten rock that hissed and steamed.

A rumble like an earthquake rippled out from the inside of the sarcophagus and across the floor. It caused a few candles to topple to the floor, some rocks to fall into the pool, and dust motes to dance just briefly enough to be noticed.

For a few moments, the cavern was still. Lazarus could hear his blood thumping through his body. Then, in that awful silence, a wet brown hand reached out from inside the sarcophagus and a dark fluid dripped from its fingers in thin slivers, spitting as it hit the white-hot rock that spilled out from the names carved into the sarcophagus.

With a creak like someone sinking into a leather chair, the fingers gripped the stone hard. A wave of liquid spilled over the edge and on to the floor, slipping across it like mercury in a tin.

Lazarus's eyes were firmly fixed on the silhouette rising out of the fluid with a terrible, deliberate momentum. Its head turned and as it let its jaw fall to speak, Lazarus saw how the thing was eyeless. God, what had they *done* . . .

'Arielle . . .'

The voice was like something slipping down an alleyway from far off, or tumbling down a mountainside. It had depth, but seemed to take flight on a breathlessness that filled Lazarus's mind with images of blackened trees being swept away by storms and lightning.

Arielle stepped forward. Her sword was no longer in its scabbard, but drawn and raised.

'Abaddon,' she said. Her voice seemed to falter a little. 'We are here in search of assistance. The Dead are on the move. And you and I know Hell will follow them. They have a weapon of some description. I . . .'

Abaddon raised a hand and shushed Arielle. Lazarus was astonished. What, in the name of everything horrific they had already seen, wielded enough power to turn Arielle to silence?

'But Abaddon—' said Arielle.

The silhouette's head creaked like the mast of a wooden ship complaining out at sea.

'Quiet, angel ...'

Abaddon rose to his full height. Almost as though he moved in slow motion, he stepped from the sarcophagus and faced them all. Fluid poured from his body for a few seconds like he'd just stepped out of the world's dirtiest shower. When it finally slowed to a drip, he walked forward, leaving a trail of footprints that reminded Lazarus of the bloody marks Red had left across the lounge carpet.

Lazarus's first thought was that if he was looking for someone, or something, to take on the Dead, then Abaddon was it. All of it. And then some. Abaddon's skin, now truly visible in the yellowy candle glow, was a dark chestnut brown that looked more like the bark of an old oak tree than leather. From the top of his ribcage to his navel, a thick, ragged black scar ran in a line that looked like it had been cut by a saw rather than a precision medical blade. And it was sewn together by thick black thread like a bootlace. Lazarus remembered Arielle saying something about Abaddon mummifying himself. Looking at the evidence in the flesh made his stomach turn.

As for the rest of Abaddon's body – for he was completely naked and seemed not in the slightest bit concerned – his head was bald, his face scarred like a bear had tried to chew it off, and on his left hand two fingers were missing. There were black holes where his eyes had once been. Abaddon was a complete mess, and utterly terrifying to behold.

Abaddon walked towards Craig, then Clair. They both looked like they were staring death in the face, all colour drained from their faces, fear beading into sweat on their skin.

Lazarus watched as the creature leant in close to each of them, almost as though he was sniffing them. Both Craig and Clair tried to lean back, out of his way, but Abaddon's awful face just pushed in closer like he wanted them to topple backwards. Craig stumbled a little and Abaddon laughed. But Clair held her ground, even when Abaddon reached out and gently caressed her cheek with the back of his hand.

Then he passed them by and stood in front of Lazarus.

'Your companions have the faint stench of the Dead on them,' he said, 'but you smell of death itself.'

Lazarus kept absolutely still. He tried not to stare, but it was impossible. Abaddon's words brought back what Red had said about death being a part of him now. Could Abaddon sense that?

Abaddon's hand came round his neck. 'You are the Keeper, boy, are you not?'

The sensation of the wet, leathery skin against his own made Lazarus's whole body crawl. The grip wasn't strangling him, but it held him fast. Lazarus nodded as best he could. He felt Abaddon's fingers flex a little on his neck, like they were trying to decide if they were going to snap it in half or not. He also reached behind for the spike, felt the thorns on the handle slip through his palm and out the back of his hand. If Abaddon tried anything, he was going to skewer the leathery freak and send him back to Red for good.

Abaddon smiled, but the rest of his face didn't follow suit. The smile sat there all alone, a cold, dark cut of night in a face of muddy brutality.

'Then tell me all,' said Abaddon, finally releasing his grip. 'Now.'

Lazarus figured it best if he did exactly as Abaddon requested.

'So,' said Abaddon, when Lazarus finished speaking, 'you have become acquainted with Red?'

It was a rhetorical question and Lazarus decided to leave it that way.

'You have not only seen the Dead, but walked their paths, tasted their world.'

Lazarus simply nodded.

'And now you have been sent to me with news of something I have known about since I was, how shall we say, born again ...'

This was news to Lazarus. 'You know of the Dark?'

'It is why Red sent you to me,' said Abaddon, and Lazarus was sure he almost bowed as he turned and walked back to the pile of rock and rubble around his sarcophagus. 'I know of the Dark. I know of what it is made. And I know of its creator. It has been a long time coming. And, sweet Arielle, I had a sense I would see you again, despite our final farewell.'

'I had no choice, Abaddon,' said Arielle. 'You were acting on your own agenda. You were dangerous. It was either trap you here, or kill you. And I couldn't really do that, could I?'

An odd sound like a bursting drain fell from Abaddon's mouth and Lazarus assumed he was laughing. So Arielle was responsible for Abaddon being trapped here, was she? He made a note to remind himself that once this was over he had to find out more about Arielle's past. The drinking was one thing, but creatures like Abaddon? What else had gone on in her life? What kind of messed up back story was she hiding from them?

Abaddon turned his glare back to Lazarus.

'I also know for what it will be used.'

'You mean you can save my father?' said Lazarus.

'That I did not say,' said Abaddon, then smiled and pointed to Craig. 'You!'

Craig shot a desperate look at Lazarus. Lazarus pulled his hand from behind his back to reveal the spike he'd kept hidden.

Abaddon was unconcerned by the threat. 'Put away

your pin, Keeper,' he said. 'If I wanted you all dead, then know that your death would be long and painful, and that by now you would already be begging me to stop. And that I would not.'

Lazarus didn't drop the point of the spike.

Abaddon swung his arm round to point at a pile of stones against the cavern wall. 'Behind there. Bring it to me.'

No one moved.

'He's talking to you, Craig,' said Arielle. 'Do as he says.'

Unable to take his eyes off Abaddon, Craig edged towards the stones and pulled them away from the wall. He removed a wooden casket clasped tight in thick, black iron bands, about the size of a large suitcase.

'To me,' said Abaddon.

Craig obeyed, dragging the casket across the floor. He was pretty much out of breath when he was done. Abaddon did not say thank you. He simply wrenched the lid from the top of the chest and flung it across the cavern. He then proceeded to dress himself in the items he pulled from the casket: large black leather boots; a black shirt over which he threw a long dark brown coat of thick oiled canvas – it looked like it was held together more by luck than needlework; a brimmed hat with tattered edges like rats had been at it; and finally a white dog collar. He went back to the casket and this time he filled up every pocket and loop and pouch on his clothes with such an arsenal of weaponry that Lazarus felt decidedly outmatched with just his spike. Abaddon had blades and knuckledusters of all sizes, and finally pulled out a roll of oiled canvas tied tightly with twine. He unravelled it to reveal so many flintlock pistols that Lazarus couldn't see how he could carry them without posing a risk to anyone around him, or indeed move at all.

'Abaddon,' said Arielle, when he'd finally finished and rolled the flintlock canvas up once more, 'you know we have called you because we need your help. You also need to understand that if you decide to go this alone, then—'

Abaddon interrupted. 'You will have no choice, correct? And we shall dance that same dance?'

'But it won't just be rocks I'll use to keep you down,' said Arielle. 'This time I'll make it permanent. There will be no coming back. I promise you that.'

Lazarus wasn't sure but it looked as though Abaddon actually smiled before he spoke again.

'Then let us not waste any more time,' he said, walking to the pool's edge, 'for there's a hunting to be done!'

And with a splash Abaddon dived into the pool, to make his unwelcome return to the outside world.

A black shard of vengeance once again on the prowl.

26

💀 EVIL DISTILLED 💀

Lazarus was thrown from the pool. Arielle had dragged him under the water to head back through the sump after Abaddon, her hand clamped tightly over his mouth. He coughed up a lungful of water and spat drool. She had a point about learning to swim, if only to stop her ever doing this to him again.

'Here,' said Craig, reaching down to help Lazarus up. 'He's already set off down the tunnel. For an old dead bloke who stinks like a dead badger, he can seriously shift.'

'Clair?'

'Here,' said Clair, swimming to the side. 'Where are the others?'

'Arielle dropped Laz and followed Abaddon,' said Craig. 'She looked almost scared.'

The cold of the water mixed with the draft skittering down the tunnel from outside. It wasn't much but it was enough to make Lazarus shiver. He almost wished he was back in Abaddon's tomb.

'Come on,' said Lazarus. 'We need to keep up with them. I don't know what Abaddon's capable of, or what he knows, but I can't help feeling if we lose sight of him that'll be it.'

As Lazarus made to lead the way down the tunnel, Craig yelled out. But it was more of a howl than a scream, like a hyena with a thorn in its paw. His eyes were squeezed tight and his body had frozen stiff.

'Craig? What's up?' Lazarus was close enough to grab his friend as he dropped to the floor holding his head. Lazarus lowered him gently to the ground.

'Is he getting those headaches again?' asked Clair, dropping next to Craig.

Lazarus nodded. 'Those tablets seemed to work,' he said. 'Got any more?'

'Why would it come back so violently?'

'You're the one with the medical background,' said Lazarus.

'My bag's still in the truck,' said Clair. 'He'll have to hang on till we get back.'

Craig opened his eyes.

'Hell, that was like someone crashed a sledgehammer into my head.'

Lazarus asked, 'What happened?'

'Everything just went black,' said Craig. 'Then my head exploded and now I'm on the floor. I was sure I was going to chuck up. I'm fine now, though. Seems to have gone as quickly as it arrived.'

'OK to stand?'

Craig nodded and grabbed Lazarus's hand.

'I'll give you something when we get back to the truck,' said Clair. 'But you need to take it easy, OK? Whatever that was, it was a serious attack. You could really hurt yourself if you collapsed and no one was there to catch you.'

'That was me by the way,' said Lazarus. 'I'm the hero.'

'Lucky me,' said Craig. 'Shall we get moving?'

As they scrambled along the tunnel – which seemed shorter this time, even the section where they had to crawl – Lazarus made Craig pause for a quick rest. Craig stopped and sat down, resting against the tunnel wall.

'Look,' said Lazarus, 'all of this . . . I'm sorry I got you into it, you know? You didn't have to stay. You could've gone home.'

'And miss all the fun?'

'I'm serious,' said Lazarus. 'I'm just saying be careful, OK? It's bad enough trying to deal with what's going on with my parents. If you got hurt as well . . .'

'You're gonna make me cry if you don't stop,' said Craig.

'You listen to a word I said?'

'Never.'

Lazarus smiled. 'Come on . . . before Arielle sends Abaddon after us.'

They soon caught up and, as they drew close to where they'd entered the cave, Lazarus tasted a change in the air from stale and stagnant to fresh and alive. With a final burst of energy he charged along the tunnel, aiming for the light he could see getting bigger and bigger. Then he was through and out into the open air and it had never, ever, smelt or tasted so good. OK, so it was pissing down, but he didn't care. He was wet from the sump pool anyway. This was outdoor wet. Mountain dew wet. The kind of wet that made you feel properly alive. Which was something to relish, he decided, considering all he'd seen and done and all that was to come.

Clair and Craig appeared behind Lazarus, splashing down the stream to meet him. Arielle was standing with Abaddon just a few metres away.

'Good to be back outside, isn't it?' Lazarus said, walking over to join Arielle and Abaddon with Clair and Craig at his side.

Abaddon didn't answer. Instead he asked, 'What do you know of the Dark?'

'Only what I saw,' said Lazarus, 'and what it did to my dad. Red told me lots of doom and gloom, but no specifics. Arielle told us a little.'

'They know from what it is made,' said Arielle. 'That is all.'

'The Dark is evil in its purest form,' said Abaddon. 'Not as an action or a person, but as a substance, a *thing*. And the moment the Dead knew of its existence, they wanted it. And now it seems they have it.'

'So where is it from?' Craig wanted to know.

'How was it made?'

'How it is created, *distilled*, is not important,' said Abaddon.

Lazarus knew right away that Abaddon was holding something back. Something Lazarus knew was important. It made him feel uneasy.

'What the Dead will do with it now they have it is our concern,' said Abaddon.

'They're using my dad to bring it to this side of the veil,' said Lazarus. 'At least I think that's what they're doing. That's why they tricked him into thinking he could get Mum back. He'd go in and they'd have him – a Keeper to fill with the Dark, with the power to open up holes in the veil whenever and wherever they wanted. Because that's the one thing they can't do unless they find a weakness there already. Right?'

'In the land of the Dead,' said Abaddon, 'the Dark has no power. It is little more than a wind blowing without purpose or direction.'

'Well it seemed pretty effective on Dad,' said Lazarus.

'Because your father, Lazarus, is a living thing,' said Abaddon. 'Arielle has told me the details of what he did, what you have all done. We have little time left.'

'Red told us to get you,' said Lazarus. 'So why don't you tell us why? What's so important about you? What is it that you know about the Dark?'

'You saw what it did to your father,' said Abaddon, ignoring Lazarus's question. 'If the Dead bring the Dark through the veil, it will have the power to swamp humanity!'

'To what end?' asked Clair. 'Why do the Dead need the Dark? What's this really about?'

'Your world,' said Abaddon, 'is what it is about. The Dead want it. And they want you – *all* of you. Fresh bodies for them to slip into, possess, use to live out every sick, crazed, twisted fantasy and idea they have in their heads.'

'A world of zombies,' said Craig. 'Except the Dead would know exactly what they're doing.'

'And we'd be powerless to do anything about it,' said Lazarus as the true power of the Dark dawned on him. 'Because the Dark is the trap, isn't it?'

'What do you mean?' asked Clair with a frown.

Lazarus's mind was on fast forward now and he couldn't

stop. 'Remember when that Dead thing was in you and you said how it was like you were trapped in a little room inside yourself, unable to do anything, but able to see everything your body was doing, even experience the thoughts and dreams of the Dead thing that had possessed you?'

'It's not something I'll ever forget,' said Clair.

'Well that's what the Dark will do, isn't it?' said Lazarus. 'It'll lock every single human it touches inside themselves, and give whichever Dead happens to be passing by a free ride!'

At that moment, the sky around them was split with a thunder crack. It exploded with such intensity that Lazarus, Clair and Craig flinched.

'Bloody hell!' Craig exclaimed. 'I've never heard it like that before.'

But Lazarus had heard more than just thunder. Behind it had been something else. Distant, but definitely there. The sound of voices yelling and shouting and hollering and screaming.

'The Dead . . .'

'What did you say, Lazarus?' Arielle said.

'It wasn't thunder.' Lazarus stared up at the sky like he was expecting the bubbling, boiling clouds to fall on them at any minute. 'It was the Dead. It was the veil being ripped apart. They're coming.'

Craig was eyes-wide. 'What here? Now?'

Lazarus nodded. 'Arielle said how they want me out of the way first, remember? They've been following us all the way. The brick through the window, the car trailing us up the motorway, the car that rammed us. This whole game of chess to get us into a corner where we can't escape.'

'But how did they track us here?' asked Clair. 'And how can you be sure?'

'Because I can smell them,' said Lazarus, and slipped the spike from his belt, the thorns piercing his hand with sudden hunger. 'But I still don't get why Red sent us to you, Abaddon,' he said. 'There's a connection between you and the Dark, isn't there? But whatever it is, you're not telling us. Not yet, anyway.'

From all around them then, the sky was sucked to an awful blackness that leaked from the horizon on all sides, like ink spreading on blotting paper.

'I don't like the look of that,' said Craig.

'I don't think you're supposed to,' said Lazarus.

The blackness crept forward. Beneath its shadow, the green lush pastures and woodland of the valley turned almost instantly to grey, like all life was being sucked from it, turning it to ash and stone and scorched earth. The sky was gone. And in its final moment, as the last shard of light was snapped in two, a figure walked out of nothingness towards them. A hooded figure all in white.

'That's the woman from the car,' said Clair. 'I just know it.'

Lazarus knew Clair was right. He also knew that this was the person he'd seen in the land of the Dead, standing beneath the frame his tortured father had been strapped to.

'It's her,' said Lazarus to himself as much as anyone who was listening, if only to confirm it. 'She's the one who took Dad.'

Craig dropped to the ground with a weak yell and this time there was nothing anyone could do to stop him thwacking his skull on the ground.

Lazarus dropped to his friend's side. 'You OK, mate? What happened?'

He could see dark blood already seeping from a deep cut on Craig's head.

'Help him!' Lazarus shouted, looking at Clair. 'He's unconscious. And bleeding!'

Clair was with Lazarus even before he'd finished speaking.

The woman let out a laugh so thin it sounded like wire slicing through the air. She was no more than a few metres away now. Lazarus could see her much clearer now than he had in the land of the Dead. Despite the shadow of the hood, he could see narrow eyes, sallow skin, a thin smile. Definitely feminine.

'Get Craig and yourself out of sight,' Lazarus told Clair, pointing away. 'Those rocks over there – hide! Don't come out. Don't move.'

'What's going to happen?' asked Clair.

'I don't know,' Lazarus admitted. 'But I've got more chance than you two of surviving it. And I don't want to have to think about saving your arses at the same time as mine, OK?'

A faint smile flickered across Clair's face. 'Be careful,' she said and she started to drag Craig away. Lazarus glanced at the spike he was holding, the thorns sticking out through the back of his hand. 'Kind of hard when I've got this, don't you think?'

Clair said no more and was soon out of view.

A shot rang out and Lazarus turned away from Clair and Craig to see smoke rising from a flintlock in Abaddon's hand. Lazarus followed the path the bullet had taken and saw a neat hole in the chest of the figure. It had no affect at all.

'I hope that's not all you've got,' said the figure.

Abaddon grunted in reply and reached for two more flintlocks.

The woman raised a hand and said, 'I have something to show you.'

She pointed. A man was walking towards them, and behind him, a crowd followed. With each step he seemed to connect with the ground like he was sinking into it, rather than walking on top of it. As he drew closer, Lazarus noticed something swirling and spinning around him. At first he thought it was just the rain blowing past, but he soon realized he was very mistaken. It wasn't the rain. It was pure darkness. It was *the Dark*. And it was twisting around the man's feet, catching on his fingers, being pulled from the air in thick ropes and twirling strands.

Lazarus glanced at Abaddon, then at Arielle. They were both staring, both armed.

'Just who the hell are you?' Lazarus shouted, looking again at the figure in white, but unable to ignore the man who approached, or the crowd that followed. He could see them clearly now. And they were the Dead. He knew who the man was. He wished he didn't, but there was nothing he could do about it. Everything was going from bad to game over.

The woman in white reached up and slipped off the hood, then pushed back her hair so Lazarus could see clearly the face she had been hiding.

Lazarus stumbled backwards.

The figure smiled. 'Hello, *love* . . .'

27
☠☠☠ FROZEN AGONY ☠☠☠

'Mum...'

Lazarus could feel all eyes on him now as he stared at the person in front of him. He didn't want to face any of them. He knew what they were thinking: that he was nuts, seeing things. But he wasn't. His mum's face was burned into his soul. He'd never forget it. His dad had made sure of that, force-feeding him on a house littered with photographs of her in every room. It was her all right. So now what was he supposed to do?

Abaddon spoke, his voice a low grumble of water and stone.

'It's a fox trick,' he said, cocking his pistols. 'Don't listen to her. Never listen to the Dead. Their words are as rotten as their gangrenous souls.'

'It's not,' said Lazarus quietly stunned with the truth

of that moment. 'It's her.'

He forced himself to stand tall in front of the woman, but inside he was crumbling. Everything hadn't just been turned on its head. It had been incinerated.

Here was the woman his dad had worshipped all his life, risked everything to see again, walked paths no living person should ever take. And now here she was and Lazarus knew the whole thing had been a trick from the beginning. His dad had been duped. And now so had he.

He felt sick. Not just because he knew all this, but because now he also knew that his mum had been responsible all along. It was she who had tricked Dad into going to find her. And it was she who had strapped him to that frame and sent the Dark into him to tear his soul apart.

Lazarus wanted to fall down and weep. But he wouldn't let himself.

'You should be dead, Lazarus.'

Lazarus couldn't remember his mum's voice. He'd been two when the accident had happened. He had no real memories of her. Hearing it now, he hoped it had sounded different when she'd been alive, because now it was a snarling thing that snapped at him.

'Why did you trick Dad?' Lazarus forced his voice out, though it was quiet and wavered more than a little. 'You've made his whole life a lie! And mine!'

His mum laughed, but even though Lazarus knew she was mocking him, he noticed something forced in the sound. Was it a hint of regret? He couldn't believe that. Not now. Not with everything going down as it was. But he couldn't ignore it either. Something in that laugh was betraying her. And all that did was push his hurt deep down and stir his rage.

'It was you in the car, wasn't it? I saw you as we drove away. How did you find us?' Lazarus didn't care how demanding he sounded. With the world gone this crazy, he wanted answers. 'How did you know we'd be here? How? We lost you. You didn't follow!'

'Your friend,' said his mum, flicking a thin finger in Craig's direction. 'It was chance, really. If he hadn't been infected by one of the Dead, then, yes, this would've been a much lengthier chase. Though we would still have found you. What luck has played out for us, Lazarus!'

Lazarus remembered the black liquid he'd seen spilling

from the creature into Craig's mouth. It had left a trace of something inside Craig which had acted as a beacon for the Dead. Lazarus felt helpless. They would never have escaped. His mum, the Dead, had always been only a few steps away.

'Your father's life was always a lie,' his mum said, 'I'm sure you know that now better than most.'

'But he loved you,' Lazarus replied and he could feel tears hot on his cheeks. The bitterness in her voice was like ice. 'When you died that was it, he was gone. He spent every day thinking about you. I lost my dad the day I lost you! Why are you here? What's this about?'

His emotions were twisting themselves into a ball. The Keeper part of him – the bit that was holding the spike, that had taken on the Dead – was charging through him, screaming at him to drive the weapon into the woman in front of him and bring her down with one swift blow before it was too late. But there was another part of him, the bit that was a son, a little boy with no mother and a lost father, and that was hurting now, battered and broken, everything it had ever thought lying in pieces at his feet. He felt like his heart would rip in two at any moment and he'd drop dead. In some ways, he hoped it would. It would have made all this a lot easier to deal with. And he still couldn't get away from how her voice had sounded, albeit so briefly. He'd heard an echo of humanity in her, he was sure of it.

'I never really wanted you, did you know that? Did he ever tell you that little truth, I wonder?'

No words could have stung worse than those. Lazarus felt like he'd been kicked in the head by a bull. If he had heard anything human in her voice, it had just been erased.

'You were your father's pride and joy, sweet Lazarus, not mine,' she said in disgust. 'He would drop everything for you, stay up all night with you when you couldn't sleep. I was as good as abandoned. '

'What are you talking about?' said Lazarus. 'Dad was always cold, distant.'

'Can you imagine how I felt when I knew Red had saved you and not me? *You*, Lazarus! A snivelling little child! Why not me? Why did you get a second chance at life, and not I?'

This was all getting very surreal. Lazarus could feel his

nerves starting to fray. Would there ever be a moment when everything felt normal and the things he'd been told didn't turn out to be lies?

'It wasn't my fault!' Lazarus yelled, jabbing a finger into his chest like a bullet. 'And you're blaming me? You're insane!'

'Lazarus . . .'

It was Arielle, but Lazarus didn't respond; he was too preoccupied with keeping a grip of his sanity.

'The figure behind her, Lazarus,' said Arielle, her voice louder this time, and with an edge to it. A threat. 'Do something now before it's too late!'

Lazarus flicked his eyes to what Arielle was talking about. For a second or two, they danced between his mum and the man who approached. The man he knew.

Behind this man the crowd of the Dead snarled and spat, and Lazarus almost lost himself to the nausea he'd worked so hard to control. He forced it back, kept himself together.

The man was almost floating now on a twisting cloud of black ribbons that danced and spun like snakes thrown on a fire. His arms were loose by his sides, his palms facing forward. But it was the eyes that held Lazarus. They burned with a black fire and wept darkness down his face. And though every part of Lazarus wished it not to be so, it was a face he recognised all too well, even though it had been twisted into a broken version of what it had been once upon a time. He'd seen it ruined on that frame. Then frozen in agony in the Dark on the moors after the crash. And now here.

Dad . . .

Lazarus was struck dumb. He couldn't move. Couldn't think.

'All I wanted, Lazarus, was a life with your father.'

There was that regret again. But it was a selfish thing, Lazarus realised. It didn't include him.

His mother seemed to become more agitated. Did she really want him dead? Why?

'Just the two of us,' she said. 'You ruined that, but I thought I could cope. Once you were old enough, I was going to ship you off to boarding school, rid myself of the burden of you.'

Lazarus's rage was building now, pushing through every other emotion he felt until all that remained inside was torrent of liquid fire.

'And then I was killed, Lazarus! Killed in a car accident! My life ripped away in an instant! Everything I wanted, everything I'd worked for, gone. And for what? For nothing, Lazarus! Nothing!'

'I was your son!' Lazarus cried back, unable to hold back burning tears. 'How can you say any of this? How can you blame me for it? I didn't kill you and I didn't get me sent back either! I've spent my life wanting a mum! How can you be doing or saying any of this?'

Lazarus was aware of the spike in his hand, and what he was capable of when he put it to use – it's terrible power, its terrible efficiency.

'I wouldn't let that be the end of it, Lazarus. No. I wanted the one thing I should have had, were it not for you and unfortunate Fate. And now I'm here to get back what is rightly mine, and to take from you what you never deserved and what I should never have given in the first place.'

Lazarus closed his eyes, allowed himself to be swept up by the rage inside him now. Whatever dream he'd had about who his mother had been, it was in pieces. No amount of glue would put it back together again.

'And look – I am not alone! We, the Dead, have come, Lazarus! We have come so that we may have life again, and live it to the full!'

'Enough with the procrastinating,' Abaddon said, and fired both pistols before pulling from inside his coat an ancient blunderbuss which exploded in a hail of acrid smoke and spinning shot.

Lazarus took advantage of the cover afforded by the cloud, and leapt through it in the direction of his mother. But he was caught sharp by a hand that grabbed him round the neck and held him high.

The smoke cleared and Lazarus saw his mum staring up at him. She grinned.

'Time for a family reunion . . .'

28
~~ THE DARK ~~

Lazarus saw the Dark sprayed out of his father's eyes. It twisted and turned on itself, enveloped Lazarus completely and started to grow, sucking darkness from all around it like it was feeding. There was no scream of agony, just the horrible silence of inevitability, as though no matter what he now did, hope had abandoned them.

Lazarus felt himself swept sideways as his mum threw him off to his left, as though he was little more than fresh road kill knocked into the gutter. He landed with a crack and looked up to see Abaddon staring down at him. At least he assumed he was staring. His face was cocked downwards to face him, but how Abaddon saw anything with no eyes, Lazarus hadn't a clue.

Abaddon grabbed Lazarus's shoulder and pulled him to his feet.

'You ready to fight for your life, Lazarus?'

Lazarus raised the spike in answer.

'Take this too.' Abaddon said, and swiftly unclipped from his belt an evil-looking scythe. The blade was rusted, but Lazarus had a feeling it was no less keen. 'It has served me well and severs with almost surgical ease.'

A moan rolled towards them.

'The Dead,' said Abaddon, glancing to where the sound had come from. 'You focus on the Dark. I will see that they come no closer. Agreed?'

'But Red sent us to you because you would know what to do about the Dark! I don't! I haven't got a clue how to beat it! The Dark is your job, not mine!'

'It is not that simple,' said Abaddon, swiftly reloading his blunderbuss as Arielle shot past them to charge at Lazarus's mother. 'We survive this, and I will tell you why Red sent you to find me. Until then, all you need to know for now is that tonight will not see the Dark destroyed. We can only delay it a while. That is all. Do you understand?'

'No, I bloody well don't!'

Had the whole thing been a wild goose chase that was

going to end up with them all being killed? Lazarus didn't know whether to give up on the spot, ram the spike into Abaddon, or just go nuts and kill anything he could lay his hands on.

'Well that matters not,' said Abaddon. 'I will tell you this – the weakness of the Dark is what lies at its centre.'

'You mean Dad?'

'Damage what lies there,' continued Abaddon, 'hurt it, and we have a chance.'

'You're mental!' Lazarus screamed. 'I'm in this to save my dad and that's it! No way am I going to risk hurting or killing him!'

'It's our only chance, Lazarus!'

'I'm not doing it!'

'Abaddon's eye sockets glared at Lazarus like search lights. 'You have little choice, Lazarus.'

He bounded off towards the Dead. They were closer than Lazarus had realised and Abaddon was soon swamped by them.

'Laz!'

It was Craig! OK, so he was awake, but Lazarus had given Clair clear instructions to stay hidden, out of sight. What the hell was Craig doing shouting out his name?

Desperate to keep his friends safe, Lazarus raced towards where they were supposed to be hiding. As he drew close, a black tentacle of the Dark shot out of the air and sent him tumbling. Another came, aimed directly at his head. He ducked, rolled left, then right. But in that split second, as the Dark adjusted its aim, Lazarus saw something.

It happened when the tentacles pulled back to spit out once more. The force of their thrust pulled the Dark open in great fissures. And at the bottom of one, stuck fast and drilled by a thousand million tendrils of black, was his dad.

Lazarus's whole world paused. His father's eyes were wide open, but, like across the rest of his body, the black tendrils drove in and out through every part of his body. Lazarus couldn't even begin to imagine the agony his father was in. Hot tears burned his skin.

A sound cracked the air and Lazarus instinctively duckedas atentacle buzzed overhead.

'Get down!' Lazarus shouted as he saw Craig's

head poke out from his hiding place. 'I told Clair to keep you both hidden! What are you doing? Get away from here now!'

Craig hesitated for a moment, then disappeared. Lazarus could tell Craig still wasn't feeling right, but he had to leave them to look after themselves. He had other things to think about now. Namely, his parents. There was no way in heaven or hell he was going to risk killing his father, no matter what Abaddon had said. He'd seen him now, and knew the terrible pain he was in. He was his dad's only hope.

A gust of wind swept across from overhead as Arielle swooped past like a great eagle. She was carrying two of the Dead. With awful precision she launched them both at his mother. The two screaming bodies piled through the air, and only missed because she was no longer where she'd been standing a second earlier. But Lazarus had spotted her. He didn't know what he was going to do, but he gave chase anyway.

Lazarus was almost on her when a thick thread of Dark whipped out of the sky and caught him hard in the stomach. He was lifted off the ground and landed on his back, his breath driven out of him. He opened his eyes to see the thing coming again. He dodged it, saw the crater it left in the ground where he'd been lying. If he hadn't moved, it would've cut him in half.

Another tentacle came, and as it reared up to come down on him, Lazarus saw another fissure open. There, once again, lay his dad. Lazarus screamed out, but the tentacle came down and Lazarus dodged it, rolling against a rock wall he hadn't even noticed. He knew immediately that he was in trouble. He was trapped. The rock wall was too high to climb, and the only way out was through the Dark. What chance had he got?

A whistle in the air and Lazarus moved again. As he did, something fell from his pocket. The wind caught it, flipped it over.

'No . . .'

It was the photograph he'd found in his dad's workshop.

Lazarus made to grab it as the wind came again, but he wasn't quick enough. It flipped over him like a gymnast.

Another tentacle. SLAM! Lazarus saw the tentacle retract, but also saw that the photograph was stuck to it.

There was nothing he could do but watch and wait and hopefully dodge the next strike.

Then something strange happened. Another fissure appeared. The tentacle with the photograph turned and slipped inside. For a second or two, nothing happened. Then ...

The fissure opened again. Lazarus could see his father. He was deep inside the Dark. Something was different. He looked in no less agony, but now, rather than just taking what was happening, he was struggling against it. It wasn't much, but Lazarus knew it was enough to give him time to escape.

He was straight up on his feet and sprinting, zigzagging as the Dark came at him again. It swept for his feet, and he skipped over it. Then it came back, this time for his head. Lazarus threw himself into a forward roll, bounced up and kept going. He didn't know where he was running to, but he figured he had a better chance of survival running than standing still. But he'd learnt something. Though he couldn't prove it, he was sure his dad had somehow seen the photograph and that had sparked something inside him, caused him to fight back. It hadn't lasted long, but the fact it had happened at all told Lazarus that his dad was still in there. And alive.

Again the Dark came for him. But before it got close, something hauled it out of the way.

'Go help Abaddon!' yelled Arielle, wrestling with more thick tentacles of the Dark that drove out towards her. 'He may not look like he needs it, but we need him more than he needs that sweet taste of revenge he's so in love with!'

'But what about Dad?' Lazarus shouted back. 'He's in the Dark! I've seen him! He's alive!'

'And Abaddon is the only person who can help him. So move!'

Lazarus went to reply but Arielle was gone, twisting through the air as more and more strands of the Dark shot after her to tangle her up and pull her down. With nowhere else to go, Lazarus gripped his spike and the scythe Abaddon had given him, and charged.

The Dead faced him with delight, their eyes wild with a desire to take his body over. Soon they weren't just fighting him, but each other, as they all tried to take him on, to get close enough to sink into his flesh and possess him. Until they realised that being touched by Lazarus was the one thing they really had to avoid.

The first to come at Lazarus ran itself through on the spike, only noticing when it was hilt-deep in its chest. The next was only slightly more cautious. Lazarus dispatched it with a deft punch of the spike through its head, followed by a swipe of the scythe taking the head from the body. Abaddon had been right – the scythe really was good when it came to severing.

Lazarus was soon lost to the fight. All he could see before him was a sea of things he was charged with sending back to where they came from. He became a machine. One after another they fell, but all Lazarus saw was red. Not just of the blood and gore now freely flowing and turning the ground beneath into a dangerous slick, but his rage that burned him for the lies he'd believed about his mother, how she'd tricked his dad, how she'd betrayed him. And the more he fought, the more his rage grew, until all that he could think about was sending his mother back to where she belonged. Perhaps even further.

All the way to Hell.

A shout from Abaddon gave Lazarus just enough of a hook to bring himself back.

'She comes!'

His mother was floating towards them, her feet planted firmly on the Dark. And lying in her arms was Arielle, either unconscious or dead.

As if ordered by some unspoken command, the Dead stopped and fell back. Lazarus didn't know what surprised him more – the number still left, or the number littering the ground in various stages of decomposition. The smell was almost tangible.

'I believe this belongs to you.' His mother tossed Arielle's body to the ground in front of him.

'Now, enough of this. End it. Now.'

Lazarus spoke before he'd had a chance to think.

'No, don't do this,' he said. 'Please . . .'

Lazarus watched his mum step closer.

'I'm asking you to stop. You don't know what you're doing, where this will end!'

'Oh, but I do, Lazarus,' said his mum, reaching out a finger to stroke an ice-cold line down his cheek.

'But I'm your son,' Lazarus replied, shuddering at her

touch. 'Doesn't that mean anything?'

The finger stroking his cheek stopped moving. His mother's stare was cold and hard, but it flickered a little. With a slow blink she squeezed out a single tear.

'You almost had me there,' she said, leaning forward in a conspiratorial whisper. 'Almost . . .'

From beneath her the Dark erupted in a spray of black ropes, all aiming straight for Lazarus. He reacted instinctively and brought the spike round in a swift arc. It cut through every single one of the ropes, sent bits of them flying in all directions, spraying him with a deep red ooze that stank like a sewer.

In the confusion of the moment, Abaddon piled into Lazarus's mother, letting off such a relentless volley of shots on the way that by the time he reached her, every single weapon was spent. But he was no match for the Dark. Another tentacle wrapped itself round him and flung him high into the air. It took just a little longer than Lazarus would've expected for Abaddon's body to land.

His mum slipped forward on the dark. 'Now it's just us, Lazarus,' she said. 'One, big happy family. So be a good boy and die for me now, OK?'

And that was the only warning Lazarus got as now both the Dark, in which he knew his Dad was lost somewhere, and his mother attacked him. First the Dark came. He dodged, swung the spike, brought it down, missed. Then came his mum, and Lazarus did the same. He soon realised that he wouldn't last long against them both. He was already seriously fatigued. His parents seemed even more intent on his death than the Dead had been.

Lazarus's emotions sparked in confusion. He knew he had no choice – surviving meant attacking his parents, but the inherent wrongness of that was ripping him apart. It wasn't fair! Why couldn't he just have a normal mum and dad? Not this! It was such a mess!

'Why are you doing this?' he screamed as the Dark swung in again and only just missed thanks to a swipe from the spike. 'I'm your son! The only one you ever had! Why do you want to kill me?'

'I told you, Lazarus,' said his mother, 'You're all that stands between me and the Dead getting us a little bit of action. We want bodies, Lazarus. Fresh ones. Nice and warm. And you're the only person we know who can stop us. Good enough reason?'

It was all too much. Lazarus fell to his knees and sobbed. 'It's not fair!' he screamed. 'Why didn't you tell me any of this, Dad? Why?'

'Very touching,' said his mum. 'Now tell me. Do you wish to die first, or would you rather follow in the footsteps of your friends over there?'

It was the last Lazarus saw of Craig and Clair. Both of them had been caught by the Dark. It was wrapped round them so tight they were yelling out in pain. Then it covered them completely and they were gone.

29

CHARRED SKIN

'Where are they? What have you done with them?'
It was just Lazarus and his parents now. No one to help him, no one to encourage him. He was completely and utterly alone.

'Your father has them,' said his mother, gesturing at the Dark. The thing was now huge: a vast, pulsating mass of blackness the size of a house. 'And they will become vessels of the Dead. It will lock them away for good and allow us to slip inside and experience once again the pleasures of life as they are meant to be enjoyed by those with sufficient imagination.'

Lazarus couldn't draw his eyes away from the Dark. Wherever he looked it changed shape, seemed at once both up close and far away, defying all perspective. Knowing that somewhere inside lay his dad made it all the worse.

'And what about me?'

'You *must* perish, Lazarus. You are too much of a risk.'

Lazarus reacted first, didn't give his mum a chance to make the first move. Dropping Abaddon's scythe, he grabbed her arm, gripped it hard and focused. She went to knock him away, but it did no good. He was stuck there now. He could feel heat under his palms.

His mum screamed and tried to pull away, but it was too late. Her skin was starting to burn under Lazarus's touch. He could see smoke. She went to scream again but Lazarus was too quick. He was on his feet and had his other hand round her mouth, muffling her voice. The thorns of the spike handle sank deep into her face.

More smoke, the smell of flesh burning. Lazarus felt blood warm on his hands. He wanted to gag, but kept his cool. No way in hell was he going to lose this, no way at all. His dad was in that Dark stuff somewhere, and now so were his friends. He had to regain control, beat the creature his mum had become. Even destroy her if it came to that.

She was squirming now, trying to break free as flames started to spread up her arm and across her face. He tried not to think about what he was doing, but knew it would definitely carry an 18 certificate.

Then before his eyes, she changed. No longer the woman in the white cowl wishing him dead, she became the mother he'd grown up with, the mother in the photos that decorated his home. A smiling woman, in love with his father. Someone he'd grown up believing loved him, too.

In shock, Lazarus pulled away the hand he'd had over her mouth. Charred skin peeled off with it, hanging like wet, bloody rags from the thorns on the spike.

'Lazarus! It's me, your mum! I'm not like what you've just seen! That's someone else! Someone controlling me!'

Lazarus shook his head. This was a trick . . . wasn't it?

'I need you Lazarus! Don't let them make me harm you! Help me!'

'I . . . don't believe you,' said Lazarus. 'I can't . . .'

'Please,' his mum whimpered. 'Sweetie . . . It's me . . . Mummy! You have to believe me!'

Every bone in Lazarus's body was screaming at him to

believe her. And as he wrestled with what his mum had said, she continued to beg for help, asking him to stop, saying she was sorry. He was crying now. The flames were still spreading and his mum kept screaming. Lazarus, desperate now, reached out to her. If she was telling the truth, then he had to help her.

In the blink of an eye, she changed back to what she had been. She spat at Lazarus, swore at him, pulled at his face with her nails, drew blood. And as Lazarus tried to protect himself, he heard her call out for the Dark. Too late Lazarus realised his mistake. She had tricked him with simple illusion.

The Dark swept towards them, but instead of going for Lazarus, it went for his mother, picking her up and pulling her into the shape of an X.

Lazarus backed off. He could see lines of red starting to appear under the white cowl, like she was being pulled limb from limb. The Dark followed him, holding her aloft.

'Now, Lazarus,' his mum said, through teeth bloodied and smashed by his spike, 'you shall see the real me!'

What happened next Lazarus knew would stay with

him for the rest of his life.

The Dark jerked hard. Lazarus saw his mother's skin split and shed, her body fall to the floor with a slap like a foot pulled out of a wet sock. For a while she just lay there, a horrid, fleshy mound, the only movement her breathing. But then the mound started to unravel itself. Lazarus fell back, staring in wide-eyed horror.

The thing building itself in front of him was nothing like his mother. Or human. It was hugely tall and thin, like a giant daddy longlegs on steroids. Sharp, barbed talons ran down what had once been legs but were now massive, multi-jointed limbs. Her head was almond-shaped, with huge pale blue eyes and a thin mouth. And her body was split top to bottom by a vast, breathing, toothed wound.

Lazarus made to move, but a thick purple tongue shot out from the wound, whipping his legs from under him. It came again and he managed to dodge it with another roll. As he tried to stand up, he caught sight of Abaddon pulling himself to his feet.

'Abaddon!' he yelled, but he knew Abaddon was too far away to hear him.

In that moment of hesitation, the limbs of the thing his mum had become pinned him to the ground, piercing his skin with a spike of bone at both shoulders. He tried to move, but the pain paralyzed him. The face of the creature leaned down towards him until its ruined nose was touching his.

'Now, *Sweetie*, you die!' it said just as an explosion of fire and shot lit the night with fire. The right limb of the creature blasted in two. Looking back over his shoulder, Lazarus saw Abaddon standing tall, blunderbuss in his right hand still smoking. With his left hand, he reached behind his back and pulled out a flintlock pistol, aimed and fired. The other limb split neatly in two.

Lazarus didn't wait for an invitation – he was on his feet, and before the creature could react, he drove the spike right into it, and gave it a fearsome twist to the right.

The thing screamed and flailed like a dog trying to walk on a frozen pond. It couldn't stand up, couldn't sit down. And then, with a shudder, bits of it started to fall off. Lazarus wasn't given a chance to stand and watch as Abaddon charged over and pulled him away.

For a few more moments, the creature thrashed about. Until, at last, it stopped.

Silence.

Lazarus stared at the thing on the ground, didn't dare move. 'You think it's dead?'

'Lazarus,' said Abaddon, 'I'm not sure it was ever really alive.'

Lazarus heard the flapping of wings, but as he looked for Arielle, he saw something else. Something happening in the remains of the creature. It was a small movement as a hand thrust itself out of the ruined carcass, and was quickly followed by another.

'She's . . . alive!' Lazarus gasped.

Abaddon raised a pistol. 'Not for long.'

But they'd forgotten about the Dark. It sent out a thick blackened tentacle, like it had just landed the catch of the day, and dragged the exhausted body of Lazarus's mother from where the creature had fallen. She was still breathing.

Lazarus watched as the Dark slipped away, taking his mother with it. He made to go after it, spike at the ready, but a leathery hand held him back.

Abaddon's voice sounded as dead as everything they'd just fought.

'It is too late,' he said, his hand squeezing Lazarus's shoulder. 'Too late by half.'

30
HUNT AND KILL

'We've lost.'

Lazarus spat the words out like they were poison. The clouds cleared above, though the rain didn't. He wondered now if it ever would.

'No, we have not lost,' said Abaddon. 'This is but a battle. It is the war we must win.'

Lazarus snatched his shoulder away from Abaddon's grip.

'I didn't sign up for a war. For any of this.'

'No one did,' said Abaddon. 'The Dead started it, though I wonder if it is something that will ever truly finish.'

Lazarus wasn't listening. At that moment all he really wanted to do was turn let his anger fly. To turn on the abomination that was Abaddon and rip him to pieces.

'Red sent us to you,' he said, in a voice without emotion. 'But what use were you? I thought ...'

'You thought,' said Abaddon, 'that I would help you bring this all quickly to an end.'

Lazarus stepped away and turned to face Abaddon. 'Whatever I thought,' he said bitterly, 'I didn't expect to lose my friends as well.'

He tried not to think about whether Clair and Craig were alive or dead. But he couldn't avoid it. Dead he could almost deal with, but alive and in agony? That was too much to bear.

The sound of wings slipping through the air brought with it Arielle. She looked exhausted, her eyes sunk deep and red in to her skull, her hair sticky with sweat and blood and grime. Fresh cuts and gashes were visible across her body like she'd just spent the last half an hour running through razor wire.

'The Dead have gone,' she said.

From a deep pocket inside her jacket she pulled out a bottle of wine, cork half out of the neck. She bit it out, spat it away and handed Abaddon the open bottle. He tipped it up and poured the red liquid into his neck, dribbles spilling down his cheeks.

'Abaddon's already given me the "we've won the battle but not the war" speech,' said Lazarus, 'so unless you've got something more useful to say, don't bother.'

'The Dark is still a threat,' said Arielle, cleaning the blade of her sword with her jacket.

Abaddon nodded. 'It has gone back through the veil, taking everything with it.'

Lazarus didn't want to listen. They were talking about his father! Whatever the Dark really was, at its heart was the only family Lazarus had. Hearing them be so cold about it angered him.

'The Dark still has my dad!' he snapped. 'The Dark opened up and I saw him!'

'You must forget him,' said Abaddon. He had passed the wine bottle back to Arielle and was now calmly checking his arsenal, cleaning, reloading.

'Like you've forgotten your family.' Lazarus didn't hide the venom in his words.

A metallic click sounded.

'Don't push me, boy,' said Abaddon. 'You could never understand what I witnessed . . . lost.'

Lazarus found himself staring down the barrel of a flintlock. The hammer was pulled back.

'Abaddon, put the pistol down. Right now,' said Arielle sharply.

Abaddon reached inside his jacket and pulled out another pistol, bring it up to aim at Arielle.

'I will not let the boy ruin my chance to finish this for good,' said Abaddon. 'I have waited too long for what I knew would eventually come.'

Arielle raised her sword.

'I could strike you down before you have the chance to pull the trigger.'

'Perhaps,' said Abaddon. 'But will you risk the life of the last Keeper?'

'I still don't understand something,' said Lazarus, staring at Abaddon down the barrel of the pistol. 'Red sent us to you, right?'

Abaddon said nothing.

'But why? It's not like what we've done has made the blindest bit of difference. If anything, it's a whole lot worse than it was before!'

'Red had his reasons,' said Arielle. 'Good and

bad, I suspect.'

'You mean this was all a trick?'

Arielle shook her head. 'Red knew that to take on the Dead and the Dark, we would need more than a little luck. Sending us to Abaddon brought with it the risk of what we narrowly just survived; leading the Dead to the only thing they are scared of: Abaddon.'

'Sounds like Red set us up.'

'He had no choice,' said Arielle. 'It was a gamble, he knew that. Sending us to Abaddon with the Dead after us meant that a fight was unavoidable. I guess he just hoped the odds were in our favour and we'd survive. Which we did.'

A cold laugh hacked its way out of Lazarus. 'Survive? What about Clair and Craig? What about Dad?'

'They are not dead,' said Arielle.

'You don't know that!'

Abaddon lowered his pistols and stowed them. 'The angel is right. They are not dead, Lazarus. Not yet.'

'So how long have we got?' Lazarus demanded. 'Hours? Days? We need to save them!'

Lazarus could feel Abaddon's eye sockets burning

into him. 'If you are taken by the Dark you are not dead until you have been given to one of the Dead and they have drained every last drop of life from your body. You are then no more than a brittle husk, and they leave you to find another host.'

'How long?' Lazarus repeated.

'It is impossible to say,' said Arielle. 'The Dark could sustain them for centuries if it wanted. And the Dead can do the same. But things are close to a finish now. An end.'

Lazarus was getting tired of the run-around.

'Just tell me!'

'Days,' said Arielle. 'That is all.'

Lazarus felt horrified and helpless. 'So we can do nothing?' he said.

'You forget,' said Arielle. 'Craig's dream, Clair's vision. Remember?'

Lazarus fell silent. He did remember. All too well. 'You said it was a vision of the Dead returning.'

'Exactly,' said Arielle. 'And doesn't that beg a question?'

After a pause, Lazarus understood. 'Where,' he said.

'We need to know *where* they'll be returning, right?'

Arielle nodded. 'Craig described houses burning yet undamaged, a black hole, people allowing themselves to be freely taken by the Dead.'

'That's hardly an X on the map, is it?'

'No. But then we don't need a map.'

Something fell into place.

'You know, don't you?' said Lazarus. 'That's why Red risked sending us to you!'

'Red had no choice,' said Abaddon. 'Even though he knew the Dead were following, he sent you to find me; the only person he knew would have any chance of finding the place where the End will begin.'

'How?'

Abaddon allowed his head to fall back and, in the soft rain, raised his hands to wash his face.

'Because, Keeper,' he said, coming back round to stare at Lazarus, 'that place your friend saw in his dream? It was once my parish.'

Lazarus felt like he'd just been cracked across the face with a cricket bat.

'Your parish? But—'

'We're wasting time,' interrupted Arielle. 'The Dark is already growing in strength. We need to find that place now.'

'How's that difficult?' asked Lazarus. 'Isn't it just an old village or something?'

'Yes and no,' said Abaddon. 'And Arielle is right. We must move.' He turned to Arielle. 'Without Red ...'

'I know,' Arielle replied. 'Trust me, I know.'

'But if it is unguarded ...'

'One step at a time, Abaddon. Worry will not solve anything.'

Lazarus was mystified. What were Abaddon and Arielle on about? What did Red have to do with the village?

Abaddon and Arielle moved off back towards the Defender. Lazarus chased after them, trying to work out why they were being so mysterious about Abaddon's old parish. The English countryside was littered with villages and towns that had been around for centuries. What was so difficult about finding this one?

Lazarus upped his pace and, at the last minute, zipped past Arielle and Abaddon, ripping the driver's door open and jumping in. The keys were still in the ignition. And, with a twist, he fired the engine. It roared into the night like a beast leaving its lair to hunt and kill.

Arielle stood in the open door to make sure Lazarus couldn't slam it shut. 'What do you think you're doing?'

'Waiting for you to get in,' said Lazarus and buckled up.

'Two things, Laz,' said Arielle. 'One, you can't drive. And two, you don't know where you're going.'

'Well you're not driving either,' Lazarus replied. 'Not now you've drunk half a bottle of wine in less time than it takes me to drink a glass of milk.'

'You're not old enough,' protested Arielle. 'Neither are you insured.'

'If carrying an angel in the back isn't enough insurance, then what is?'

Arielle had no response to that.

'And as for where we're going, why are you being so mysterious about it? What's the problem?'

Lazarus turned at the sound of the passenger door being pulled open. Abaddon squeezed himself into the passenger seat.

'My parish cannot be found on any map,' he said. 'Not any more.'

'You mean it's just a ruin?'

Abaddon shook his head.

'He means,' said Arielle, 'that in this world, his parish no longer exists.'

'What?'

Lazarus couldn't understand what he was hearing. How could they find a place if it didn't actually exist?

'The whole village was damned,' said Abaddon. 'Everyone and everything sucked from this world into the next.'

'You mean it's in the land of the Dead?'

'No,' said Abaddon. 'I do not.'

'Then where?'

Lazarus felt himself pulled round to face Arielle. She didn't look as tired as she had in those moments after the Dark had left them. But her eyes held in them a knowledge of something awful. And Lazarus knew what she was going to say before the words slipped from her mouth.

'Hell, Lazarus. The village is in Hell.'

The adventure continues in
Book 3 of The Dead:

THE DAMNED

Coming soon in 2011

Read on for a sneak peek . . .

Five years ago . . .

James Barton, accountant, collector of original Star Wars toys and father of two young boys, hurled himself into the lake water, dragging himself through it with great sweeps of his arms, using them like paddles on a steamer. Waves scattered from him in great white bursts of water, dancing in the bright summer sun like bits of broken glass. And just ahead, only a few metres now and getting closer every second, floated the girl.

Please don't be dead. Oh God, don't let her be dead . . .

It was early still and he'd been out for his usual morning run when he saw her. She looked no older than ten, but he wouldn't be able to tell for sure until he got to her. Why was it taking so long? And what on earth was she doing here in the first place? Where were her parents?

James waded on. He could now make out what she was wearing. It was a simple white dress, and her arms were naked, her feet bare. But at least she was face upwards, he realised, seeing her jet-black hair curling around her in the water like the snakes of Medusa.

With a final heave, James hurled himself across the final stretch of water between himself and the girl and wrapped his arms around her, hauling her out of the cold water and into his arms. He clasped her close, forced himself not to cry out.

Please don't be dead . . . Please kid, whoever you are . . . don't . . .

James turned back to shore, the girl over his right shoulder. She felt so cold against him, and so helpless. It reminded him of how his own children felt when they fell so deeply asleep that he could just lift them up and take them anywhere without waking. Moments like that he wished could last for ever. He'd taken those memories and locked them away, sometimes bringing them out again to cheer himself up, usually when he was at work wishing he was anywhere but.

James shivered, but was nearly out of the water now. The girl was growing heavier the closer he got to dry land, but he wasn't going to let her fall. He felt strangely protective of her, as though wading in to grab her and rescue her had given them a bond that went beyond simple acquaintance.

The squelch of his soaking trainers on the shore made James realise he was out of the lake now. He turned for his cabin and ran like he'd never run before, legs cold and numb but pumping hard. Breath steamed from him, his wet shoes threatened to send him on to his face, but he kept going. At his cabin, he crashed through the door and stood for a moment, wondering just what the hell he was supposed to do now. Then he laid the girl on the sofa.

Some break this was turning out to be, he thought, as he quickly pulled from his brain all the first-aid knowledge he possessed. At the same time he scrambled across the floor to his jacket in the corner, found his phone, dialed 999.

He did all the checks, made sure the girl's airway was clear, answered the voice on the end of the call he'd punched in.

'Yes, I've done all that ... Temperature? Bloody freezing, what else? She's been in the lake, dammit! No, she's not breathing ...'

Something caught his eye. Movement.

'Just a minute ...'

James stared at the girl's chest. Yes, it was moving. Slowly, but it was moving.

'She's breathing! Yes, I'm sure! OK, I'll keep her warm. How long for the ambulance? That's fine.'

He hung up. Chucking the phone back to his jacket, James was up and through to his bedroom. He tore off the duvet and brought it back to cover the girl on the sofa. Yes, she was definitely breathing now. All he had to do was keep her warm until the paramedics turned up.

Relief flooded through James with such force he had to steady himself against the side of the sofa. He felt dizzy and exhausted and was shivering from the cold or the experience, or both.

Watching the girl lying so quietly brought home to James just how silent the cabin was without the rest of his family there with him. He was only away for the weekend for a bit of 'me' time. He had found this log cabin last-minute, on the shores of a secluded lake with free fishing. It was stunning and tranquil. But he still missed his family. It made him wonder again about the girl and how she'd ended up in the lake so early in the day. And so alone.

A cough.

James looked over to the girl.

Another cough.

'Er . . . hello? I'm James. I pulled you out of the lake. Are you OK? What were you doing there?'

James knew he was talking too much. He stopped.

The girl's eyes gazed at James like pools at the bottom of a waterfall, deep and dark and silent.

'Hi,' said James. And smiled.

The girl smiled back. 'Hello. Where am I?'

'This? Oh, it's my cabin,' replied James. 'You were in

the lake. I pulled you out. Where are your parents? I've called an ambulance.'

The girl moved a hand from under the duvet. 'The air smells so fresh. Alive.'

'Yes I suppose it does,' said James, a little taken aback. 'You need to rest. Help is on its way. But if you could tell me where your parents are ...'

'They're coming,' said the girl. 'We all are.'

The girl's hand slipped across his wrist. For a second he thought nothing of it. Perhaps she just wanted reassurance. But as she squeezed, the force of it took his breath away.

'That's hurting me,' said James. 'You don't need to be afraid. I rescued you. Look, my name's James, OK? I'm your friend.'

'They're coming,' said the girl again. She sat up, swinging her legs out to rest her feet on the floor.

James stumbled backwards. The grip she had on his wrist felt like she'd glued herself to him. Maybe it was the shock of all this that was making him think that. Yeah, that was it.

'You can let go now,' said James. 'Look, I'll get you a drink or something.'

The girl cocked her head to one side. Then, before James had a chance to react, she spun him round on the floor to face away from her, and clasped the sides of his head with her hands.

James felt like his head was on fire. He could smell burning. He tried to pull away but couldn't move, reached up with his hands to pull the girl off, but her fingers . . . No! It was impossible! They were in his face! Sunk deep into his skin, crawling down his cheeks.

James screamed. He bucked and shook and kicked. The girl just held him tight. As his world faded to black, he heard her voice one last time before finally passing out.

'They're coming,' she said again. 'They all are.'

☠☠ ACKNOWLEDGEMENTS ☠☠

Each time I finish a book I think, 'Now where the hell did all that come from?' Imagination, I reckon, is a scary thing; it sits all quiet in the background, waiting for you to poke it with a stick. Then, if you poke hard enough, it doesn't just show its teeth, it rips your face off. And smiles.

But my imagination isn't enough. A few people keep me going through the ups and downs, the elation and the self-doubt, supply coffee and doughnuts, inspire, ask the right questions, tell me how it is . . . or just sit quietly. So here's to them:

Su: Without whom . . .

Paul Edwards: No one else I know gets as excited as you do about *Suspiria*, *Phantasm* and *City of the Dead*. Or consumes as may crisps in the watching.

Acknowledgements

John and James: For doing what brothers do best and never taking anything I've ever said or done seriously. Until now, perhaps.

Kirsty Coupe: For keeping me in caffeine during those terrible days ...

Mum and Dad: Holidays in Kentmere reading *Swallows and Amazons* ...

Alan Garner: *The Weirdstone of Brisingamen* was the first book I didn't just read, but experienced. That's where all this began.

Naomi Pottesman: For taking on *The Dead* in the first place.

Everyone at Hodder who's had anything to do with this: You people rock!

ABOUT THE AUTHOR

DAVID
GATWARD

Previous job: Salmon Farmer
Loves: Horror movies
Hates: DIY
Fact: Seen two ghosts

David was born in Bristol and grew up with his two younger brothers between the Cotswolds, Wensleydale and Lincolnshire. Aside from having a huge number of hobbies including: caving, camping, climbing, archery, shooting and music, David also wrote avidly. Although he had his first book published aged 18, it's taken many more years and life experiences to lead to writing *The Dead*. Seeing two ghosts, being mistaken for a homeless person and almost drowning have given David plenty of food for thought, but it's his family who've been a big inspiration. Now living in rural Somerset with his wife and two boys, David writes full-time and hopes to see ghost number three very shortly.

Questions and Answers
with David Gatward

What do you enjoy most about writing a book?

You're playing God! Seriously – you're immersed in a world that you created, running around with characters you dreamt up, battling evil … and winning! When you realise the story is working, that the characters are as real as they could get, you find the story just starts racing ahead and you have to keep up. It's strangely exciting, a bit weird and scary, and completely enthralling. I cannot express how lucky I am to be in a position to be writing books. It's astonishing.

What do you least like about writing a book?

The fear of knowing you've got to come up with a story can be terrifying – the fear of the blank page/screen. Those days when nothing happens in your head, when it takes hours and hours and hours to come up with just a few hundred words, and each one of them really, really hurt. Deadlines approaching too fast. The fear of failure haunting you with each book you write, that it'll be total junk and the world will laugh at you and force you to wear pants on your head for the rest of your life.

Writing seems to be a very solitary occupation – are you someone who's comfortable with his own company?

Yes. But that doesn't mean I'm a hermit in a cave with a crab as my only mate. Writers need solitude to get on with it. But I've trained myself to find that anywhere (I wrote a book on train journeys over a period of five weeks). I write with the world blocked out, but when I'm not writing I love being around the people that make my life fizz and buzz and thump.

What was your favourite book as a child?

The one which sticks with me is *The Weirdstone of Brisingamen*, by Alan Garner. It has this one bit in it, where the heroes end up crawling through a water-filled tunnel and they have no choice but to go through it, not knowing if they'll get out or drown. It still haunts me today!

Have you ever seen a ghost?

Yes, I have seen a ghost. Well two, actually. The first, a man dressed all in black, appeared one sunny morning while I was mowing a lawn. Didn't say much; just stared. Kind of freaked me out though. The second, a woman in a blue dress, woke me up in the middle of the night while I was living in a caravan (which, just so you know, was situated on what was once an old graveyard). Pretty weird, particularly as, despite it being dark out, inside, the caravan was all lit up.

Who are your heroes?

I don't have any in the conventional sense, but I do have a few people I admire. These include (in no specific order): my dad, an old friend Michael Forster, and writers Linda Chapman and Neil Gaiman.

What do you do in your spare time?

As I'm making the transition from full-time yawn-filled job, to full-time 'WOW!' writing, I don't really have spare time! But in the bits I find, I hang out with family/friends, read, listen to music, cook ... and try to work out if I'll ever have time again to do stuff like play the drums, go climbing, go to the gym ...

What's your guilty pleasure?

Glee!

What's your dream car?

Landrover Defender 110 King Cab (done out to my own spec, obviously).

If you were a superhero, what would your power be?

The ability to fly. That sense of freedom, to be able to just take off and zip through the sky ... I'd so totally love that.

What is your perfect sandwich?

Er ... well, this is the one I have late at night: peanut butter, mayonnaise, Danish blue cheese, sliced onion, and cheese and onion crisps. Yeah, I know ...